P9-DBT-206

Praise for Sergio De La Pava and
A Naked Singularity

"One of the 10 best fiction books of 2012." —*Wall Street Journal*
"One of the best books of the year." —*Toronto Star*
"One of the best books of 2012." —*Houston Chronicle*
"One of the best of 2012." —*Philadelphia City Paper*

"*A Naked Singularity* is not about physics. It's about the American criminal justice system in a large and chaotic city, a place slowly crushed by hopelessness in the same way that an ancient star is gradually crushed by gravity.... The novel is a cross between *Moby-Dick* and *Police Academy*. Between Descartes and Disneyland. Between Henry James and Henry Winkler." —Julia Keller, *Chicago Tribune*

"A propulsive, mind-bending experience.... The novel's chaotic sprawl, black humor and madcap digressions make it a thrilling rejoinder to the tidy story arcs portrayed on television and in most crime fiction." —Sam Sacks, *Wall Street Journal*

"Sometimes buzz can be a good thing. Sergio De La Pava's *A Naked Singularity* is a case in point.... *A Naked Singularity* is ... a great American novel: large, ambitious, and full of talk.... We can be thankful that this time the buzz did its work." —*Toronto Star*

"Even while the lives it describes are often bleak, the book is funny, consistently so.... The heist is discussed so exhaustively that when it finally transpires it's thrilling. Casi's defendants, all messes, are lovely and authentic.... It's a fine thing for an author to bring forth something so unapologetically maximalist."
—Paul Ford, *Slate*

SPRINGDALE PUBLIC LIBRARY
405 S. Pleasant
Springdale, AR 72764

"Exuberant, hyperverbal ... a minor masterpiece of humor, paranoia, and even flashy technique." —*Philadelphia City Paper*

"One of the best and most original novels of the decade.... If you like *The Wire*, if you like rewarding, difficult fiction, if you like literary, high-quality artistic and hilarious yet moving novels that are difficult to put down, I can't recommend *A Naked Singularity* enough." —Scott Bryan Wilson, *The Quarterly Conversation*

"A fine encyclopedic romp in the Joyce/Pynchon/Wallace tradition, one with an effortless flow and arresting setting: the American judicial system as vortical funhouse." —Miles Klee, *The Notes*

"A work of amazing breadth and humor.... Challenging, addictively entertaining and not to be missed, *A Naked Singularity* heralds the arrival of a tremendous talent." —*Shelf Awareness*

"A beautiful monster of a book, a novel that left this reviewer, at least, feeling like maybe there's some point in reading novels—and writing them—after all." —Paul LaFarge, *Barnes and Noble Review*

"Sergio De La Pava brings linguistic energy and grim hilarity to this furious novel about the dysfunctional criminal-justice system. His novel evokes such maximalist masterpieces of the 1970s as Robert Coover's *Public Burning* and William Gaddis's *J R*—he has Coover's rage and Gaddis's ear—yet also grapples with current issues hot off the AP wire." —Steven Moore, author of *The Novel: An Alternative History*

"A masterpiece.... It propels the reader into a literary maelstrom worthy of Pynchon and Gaddis.... A book of unsettling oddness and power." —Steve Donoghue, Managing Editor, *Open Letters Monthly*

PERSONAE

Sergio De La Pava

PERSONAE

A Novel

The University of Chicago Press

Chicago and London

SPRINGDALE PUBLIC LIBRARY
405 S. Pleasant
Springdale, AR 72764

The University of Chicago Press, Chicago, 60637

Copyright © 2011 by Sergio De La Pava.

All rights reserved. No part of this book may be reproduced or
transmitted in any form or by any means, electronic or mechani-
cal, including photocopying, recording, or by any information
storage and retrieval system, without permission in writing
from the copyright owner.

University of Chicago Press edition 2013

This is a work of fiction. Names, characters, places, and inci-
dents either are the product of the author's imagination or are
used fictitiously, and any resemblance to any actual persons,
living or dead, events, or locales is entirely coincidental.

Printed in the United States of America

22 21 20 19 18 17 16 15 14 13   1 2 3 4 5

ISBN-13: 978-0-226-07899-1 (paper)
ISBN-13: 978-0-226-07904-2 (e-book)
DOI: 10.7208/chicago/9780226079042.001.0001

Library of Congress Cataloging-in-Publication Data

Pava, Sergio de la, author.
  Personae : a novel / Sergio De La Pava.
  pages cm
ISBN 978-0-226-07899-1 (paperback : alkaline paper) —
ISBN 978-0-226-07904-2 (e-book)
I. Title.
PS3616A9545P47 2013
813'.6—dc23
                    2013016557

♾ This paper meets the requirements of ANSI/NISO
Z49.48-1992 (Permanence of Paper).

For Claudia
and

In Memoriam:
Jesus De La Pava
John Forsythe
Antonio Mellado
Ricardo Ochoa
and
Nestor

Book Two

Pero mira cómo beben
los peces en el río.
Pero mira cómo beben
por ver a Dios nacido.
Beben y beben
y vuelven a beber.
Los peces en el río
por ver a Dios nacer.

Traditional.

I

Our Heroine and Her Work

The ensuing is the report of one Detective Helen Tame. I am Helen Tame, the ensuing is my report, and it is not true that this second sentence adds nothing to the first. I should note at the outset that this Department is obsessed with reports and I am not; if I had to cop to any obsession it would be with Truth. Truth in its multifarious instantiations, ranging from simple if inviolable mathematical truths to other less evident yet persistently attractive ones. How it is *true* that a three-year-old's smile is an unambiguous good whereas decades later those same lips must first be parsed, how certain narrative memories will attach to an extant piece of music and refuse to ever again let go, but mostly how an unexplained human death nonetheless retains a core truth that can be teased into discovery. What I do is make these discoveries then, because of the above-mentioned obsession, write about them:

The apartment I responded*fn* to was a Manhattan special,

fn. Despite the admittedly unconventional nature of this report I nonetheless intend to occasionally pepper this account with the kind of tortured locutions often found in official law enforcement documents. Thus, as in above, I will not merely go to or arrive at a location, rather I will *respond* to it in my *vehicle* (car). Likewise expect possibly copious mentions of *perps, vics, subjects, suspects, wanteds*, etc. My motivation for this I'll keep to myself but I must consequently implore the reader not to prematurely impugn my intellect nor should said reader be dissuaded from continuing with what promises to be an altogether rousing narrative.

meaning you cannot believe a human being who is not incarcerated is not entitled to more space. I am here because of blood, blood that makes little sense. John Doe is on the kitchen floor but Mr. Doe is so obviously and severely weathered, so far along his now conclusive personal timeline, that his status as a DOA would occasion no mystery remotely warranting the tentatively solicitous phone call I received but for, again, the blood.

There is blood just above the molding in the hall leading to the kitchen and less in other spots but none in the kitchen. P.O. Avery is correct and seems pleased.

"They said call you in these instances, just this morning in fact." I say nothing because I'm mildly curious what he will add. The resulting silence causes him stress he's unaware of and he says, "I took the number down. Everybody was kind of taken aback you know? Since day one it's been call crime scene, you know, don't touch anything just call. Then suddenly today it's call you instead *if attendant circumstances suggest that a high degree of notoriety will attach to the case or resolution of the matter will prove particularly thorny,* that last part starting with attendant my sergeant read from a piece of paper, he doesn't talk like that."

I am slowly walking throughout the apartment and while it is true I can attend to two matters at once, that is, I can listen to Avery's noise and still begin making the necessary observations and thoughts, I would prefer not to, that the thoughts may be richer, and for that I will have to speak. I turn to look at him directly. His pupils dilate and he has somehow managed to bore me further. He is still talking.

"I told him I had to disagree you know? Don't get me wrong, he's a great partner and all," he is glancing at him in the hall, maybe thinking *great* was too strong. "But I told him that I think this is exactly what they were talking about this morning with the thing with the attending circumstances. Because I think that's blood, fresh blood at that, and yet it doesn't appear to have come from the body, the deceased, the *decedent* I mean."

"Stop talking," I say, and he does. I am putting on gloves I designed years ago, gloves that only became the industry standard once I relented and let my name attach to them even though their physical makeup changed not in the slightest between reluctance and acquiescence, and staring at a clean spot on the carpet. "You can go now," I add, but he hesitates. "That means *leave* in Etiquette."

"Just that, well, they didn't really say what to do after calling you. In other words, does calling you, uh, *obviate* the need to call CSU? Do I fill out a report?"

"Likely."

"Nothing about what constitutes proper procedure from here on out you know? So I'm at a bit of a loss."

"More than a bit I'd say, so here's a chance for some gain. You weren't given further procedure because this is the end of the line for you. Once you call me and, more importantly, I come, then I alone make the determination of what *constitutes,* as you say, proper procedure going forward. Make sense?"

"Yes."

"So I am repeating my invitation to you to join your partner in the hall, then the street, then your RMP, to continue providing service and protection."

"Accepted."

"Well done."

"With permission to add that when I started I told myself that to the extent I made errors they would be errors of commission and not omission."

He'd made the relevant O a little too long during which I diagnosed ambition and felt remorse. "You did well officer," I say. "It *is* blood and in highly suggestive locations, good work." I then take him by the elbow like a child, a quite involuntary sin of condescension that requires I atone by asking who his sergeant is then indicating I will deposit positive impressions there, and take him to the hall where I close the door before the partner can even form the intent to speak.

Now I'm tired. Even minimal social niceties exhaust me and the commitment to future such interactions doesn't help. I am walking about the apartment collecting. I touch nothing, I am collecting observations and placing them in my mind. Once they've all been crowded in I'll order them, connect them where appropriate, delete the irrelevant, promote the critical, and begin the circuitously ineffable process of forming conclusions.

The apartment is essentially two rooms. In one, a kitchen with a refrigerator and oven that look like toy models opens into the maybe two-hundred square feet of combination living/dining room. The other is the bedroom, notable at first blush primarily for the absence of any bed frame for the mattress on the floor in the corner. Bathroom of toilet, sink, shower, ends the tour, with only the medicine cabinet intriguing me and not greatly.

Can't say the same for other things I've seen, however. For example, the main room has a piano and not a bad one. The same man who slept on the floor owned a piano. But not a television or computer. There's a radio, old as sin, the kind that looks like it was manufactured to report on the progress of the Allies. The sofa facing it has recently been cleared of considerable clutter. Not so the coffee table which seems almost comprised of newspapers and magazines. The carpet is wall-to-wall and gold with the clean spot I mentioned.

I go to the kitchen and the body on its floor. The body is splayed almost prototypically, the right arm reaching up as if hoping to be called on. In the withered hand an open orange bottle of pills, pills on the ground, pills in the yawning mouth.

No label on the bottle, no identifying features on the pills. Left hand palm-down on the floor near his waist. Medium-sized white tee shirt and pajama pants, nothing else. Eighteen pills total between bottle, floor, and mouth. Right side of face on the floor so I put a digital thermometer in his left ear. Beep and eighty-two degrees confirms he's been dead an hour and forty minutes. I squeeze his left thigh and estimate the density of his femur. I look at his face and open the eyes to see their reddish scleras.

He is more than a century old; was.

I walk away, to the other side of the counter where I sit on a stool and look into the kitchen. I forgot to close the eyes and now he is staring at me. The last thing he saw was dirty cracked linoleum but follow his eyes now and you can reach the Sun.

Someone is at the door. As they come in I stand and move away from the counter. There are steps you can take to stand in plain view without being seen, just as you can follow someone quite closely without them noticing, provided you understand the behavior of soundwaves and take care to maintain proper angles.[fn]

A tall woman walks in. She is leading a girl by the hand. They are dressed in almost costume plainness and as they pass the kitchen they merely glance at the body before entering the room I'm in. I contemplate speaking but decide I don't want to influence events, just want to see what will develop in my absence.

They are looking for something but the girl is merely mimicking the adult without comprehension. She is nine or ten.

[fn]. This is fact not opinion. For a more extended discussion of the applicable phenomena see, if even possible, Dr. Helen Tame's article *Sound Without Fury: Soundwave Behavior and Surreptitious Audition* in Issue Three of the now-defunct SCIENCE FACTION MAGAZINE.

After the woman opens and closes a drawer the girl will then reopen and close that same drawer without looking in. They are done and go into the bedroom holding nothing. I have not been seen.

In the bedroom they engage in the same conduct with the same result. They say nothing but look at each other often. The woman puts her hand to the child's face and, with a thumb, wipes her cheek. They sit on the mattress, saying nothing, holding hands. When they rise the girl is holding something and I, who have stared continuously at her face since first locking on to it well, cannot account for the acquisition.

It is a white package and it is secured shut by twine in the form of a bakery box. She is carrying it and they are walking towards me. I decide to let them see me and to investigate, I am interested. Then I step aside and they walk past. They walk past the kitchen. The woman stares straight ahead as they pass but the girl drops her head back to look. They open the door and leave. I stare at the door. Time passes. I go to the window but see no one. I have made my first mistake in a long time and that excites me with possibility.

There is nothing that blatantly indicates where the white box came from. The piano bench, for example, doubles as storage but is sufficiently full that there was no possible room for the box the girl carried so forlornly. In the bench is a notebook. A music notebook with ledger lines forming grand staffs. Written by hand, in pencil and recently, is an aria I recognize immediately but have not played in years. I take off my gloves and sit at the bench. I play it straight through once, at first using his music then from memory, the notes surprising and moving me as I remember why I stopped playing them. Then again, but this time more deliberately, allowing some notes to fade to near silence before being replaced. I begin a variation out of order then stop. The aria is the only music in the notebook. This is a coincidence but coincidences don't impress me or cause me the slightest wonder.

The average person greatly underestimates the frequency of what they term coincidence and often the unscrupulous profit as a result. Thus the frequent *discoveries* that the Bible, for example, has a hidden code that prospectively details the precise unfolding of the Franco-Prussian War or whatever until someone, one hopes, points out that the real shock would be if the comparison of two immeasurably rich entities like the Bible and all of human history failed to produce any matching patterns whatsoever. Similarly, I have mentioned that Mr. Doe spent more than a century on our planet and I fairly recently concluded my fourth decade therein creating ample opportunity for something like my having written extensively on the only piece of music transcribed by the individual whose death I'm investigating; this is especially so when one of the individuals has been a compulsive producer of monographs on wildly divergent topics, although with a discernible if not exclusive focus on matters related to investigative techniques and Music, since the age of sixteen.

And there remains the matter of the box because while it is true that the girl carried it towards the front door she did not in fact leave with it and it now rests bluntly near that door where I direct stares at it as I resume playing and pretend that what I see is a residual image not yet dissolved behind my eyes and not one supported by actual presence, a pretension necessitated by a kind of urgently palpable aura emitted by the object; how I've determined that the round pills are not responsible for John Doe's pose but almost certainly the contents of the box somehow are, all meaning that I am duty-bound to approach the box but so do not want to that I contemplate the abandonment of that duty and incorporated within is the conclusion that while such an abandonment can be perfectly legitimate it can only be so if it is not specific to this incident but is, as it were, General, meaning just the kind of complete abdication and cessation I am not even remotely prepared to make, so instead I go to the box.

I am tentatively untying the box and sitting on Doe's sofa. Wait. Should I untie the box?

I have yet to fully inhale the apartment as I eventually must, but sometimes sensing is enough and I sense that whatever secrets exist therein will devolve freely under even minimal scrutiny; not so for the box.

Should I open it?

Maybe the box is empty. I'll open it and contrary to all intuition and sense impressions reveal not a saturated piece of our universe but rather the absence at the core of everything, that what is fashionable to believe has fashion only because true.

But when I open it I'm only slightly surprised by what I see. Another notebook but this one's marble and thus spongy in the way only those can become. Initially black now barely grey, it contains writing that ranges from colorful immediacy to mere ghostly impressions.

Digging further results in an untimely TV GUIDE (yes, the mini booklike magazine) this one remarkable at first glance only for its copious writing in red ink in seemingly every available margin that once provided respite from the publication's incestually suggestive coverage of the titular industry. This writing is in the same *hand* as they say as marble notebook's.

Next is a roll of paper towels, but not the kind you would ever find in someone's home with the heightened absorbency and easily perforated sections. No, this is brown paper closer in the spectrum to wood than most paper dares, and what on introduction appears to be meaningless scribbling, thereupon evolves on closer inspection into more writing, again with the from the same hand thing, but writing made almost indecipherable by the fact that it has been quite literally rolled over itself, so that the reader's visual processing of the most immediate letters is undercut by the many successively fainter letters that constitute later writing and which essentially bleed through the paper to compete with the more relevant letters, at least when the roll is in its most composed state.

Last, is a collection (collected, at least in the nonhuman sense, by a binder clip in the upper left corner and this clip is of the largest size commonly available in the U.S.) of research. The bright whiteness of this recent paper is sudden and intense and it takes time to notice that what signifies here is not so much the computer-generated symbols on the front but, instead, the by now familiar and severely human prose on the back of almost every page.

All this represents work. Writer needs to be officially called in but I am reluctant to do so without concrete answers and I'm getting tired and it's getting dark and, truth is, the epistemological scenery of that space, the various distances and positions, etc., will not change significantly; what *will* change is the person charged with interpreting that scenery, assuming she reads everything before her. I start with the notebook.

Now it is hours later, maybe the next day, and I have read everything before putting it all back in the box, exactly as I found, it then retying said box and writing something of my own.

I'm tired.
  I have done what I can.
  I am only one person.
  Any person will be imperfect.
  Blood everywhere.

The sofa is warm and soft.

It's a big world, cold and hard, and at some point someone will lie lifeless on every inch of it.

I am only one person and I am tired.

I close my eyes.

II

1st of 3 Excerpts of Dr. Helen Tame's Introduction to Her Article: *Bach, Gould, and Aconspiratorial Silence* [fn]

In the beginning Man had fur. And his stomach hurt. It hurt and in a way mostly foreign to now. And there was sound and noise and even Music but when your stomach hurts, if it hurts enough, then sound is just sound and it doesn't arrange into beauty or meaning. What you want then is for the pain to stop. For it to not follow you wherever you go and for it to not reduce everything to need and fear.

Turns out opposable digits help do this. They eventually hold tools and it is tools that will ultimately tame the world.

In this world birdsong now registers, the accidental melody of wind through gaps in wood is for the first time truly heard and it is pleasing and pleasure that consists of more than mere pain-avoidance is then seen as a good to be actively sought and the discovery that man need not wait for happy accidents but can himself replace the bird and the wind of course not only

[fn]. Originally published in *The American Journal of Musical Theory* (Fall 2000, Vol. 93, No. 3) with an explanatory editor's note referencing the author's "singular history" including the acclaimed concert career and its unexplained abrupt cessation, all in seemingly defensive attempt to justify the odd effect the article would likely have on the journal's usual readers.

results in a great increase in that kind of pleasure but also by necessity gives prominence to those who best produce and arrange the pleasurable sounds so that significant human energy is now devoted to improving the production of these sounds initially focused on the necessary tools but later includes the realization, a big one, that the sounds have essentially hidden relationships to each other and thus to their listeners, relationships that can be broken down into kind of loose rules that while loose cannot be overstated when it comes to importance because it turns out that knowing these relationships/rules even if only intuitively and even if only to disregard them is like possessing a key (sorry) that opens precisely the doors you want opened and all this makes Music the kind of thing that can be studied and preserved, which activities give more of that prominence I mentioned to those who have skill or ability or talent or however you choose to denote the ineffable quality that allows some to order the sounds of our world into magic and it turns out, perhaps surprisingly, that a sole magician is preferable, in terms of not only effectiveness but certainly mystique and similar concerns, to collaboration, so that things like collective chants without an identifiable sole author would have to defer to the individual striving to order our chaos by sweetening our air.

And in Eisenach, Germany, in an ordinary house, on March 31, 1685, to a family steeped in Music, Johann Sebastian Bach was born.

|||

In Which Painstakingly Restored Aphorisms
Are Aired after Dormant Decades

A word here about what was in the box and how I've chosen to present it. First, the contents of said box are highly relevant to the instant investigation and as such I have decided to not merely catalogue and voucher said items but rather to present them here in their entirety. The works are here presented in chronological order, meaning in the order they were written with oldest first and most recent last. Of the chronology established and that the items represent the willful sum of Writer's effort is beyond meaningful doubt, but a brief word on the methodology used in dating the works seems warranted.

So what most directly follows is taken from the significantly aged marble notebook recovered. The manufacture date of the notebook is helpfully listed as 1970 and this date has been generally confirmed by various analyses. More significantly, almost all the writing contained therein is in pencil. Contrary to generally accepted belief (yes, again) it is absolutely possible to date lead pencil markings as will be conclusively demonstrated in a forthcoming monograph that was initially underwritten by the Smithsonian Institute then only generously completed out of a sense of professional obligation in the absence of explicitly promised funds. This dating confirms that the contents of the notebook predate the three other works recovered from the box and does this by quite a bit.

Thus, the notebook can be seen as a kind of warming up to the subsequent works that form the greater part of this report. The short story, play, and either unfinished novel or novella that follow in many ways *result* from the notebook. That the gestation depicted therein appears to have taken decades, while certainly highly suggestive, does not alter the fundamental relationship between notebook and offspring.

Lastly, the sad fact that only a portion of what was placed in the notebook has been recovered. Various forms of damage, over time, befell the notebook. It was never the highest quality paper to begin with and pencil starts fading the moment it hits such paper. In many cases, what is displayed here is the result of various techniques designed to uncover the lost. So, for example, the many instances where what was once clear and distinct devolved into invisibility, but not quite because the impressions remained: tiny canals dug into the sheets and still readable once magnified and interpreted. Predictably, the result often feels fragmentary or inchoate, perhaps heightening the effect that what we have here are halting steps towards future cohesion. All by way of maybe apologizing for the imminent lack of symmetry, narrative propulsion, cheap suspense, or any of the other décor generally sought by eyeballs like yours:

... write because of an aesthetic impulse to order the world into greater attractiveness, which ordering ...

English is richer than Spanish, just is, and I want primarily to be rich.

Art seems at least a subspecies of Love because in Art we sense Love's greatest response yet to Life's inherent cruelty.

I do not like to talk about what I've written, I do not like to talk about how or why I write, I do not like to talk about myself, what I've seen and done or what it's like to be me now, I do not like to talk.

Joseph Conrad was twenty-one before he even heard English. Twenty-one. Conrad!

Now that you're found, I'm lost.
Now that you feel love, I don't.

. . . the selfsame beauty runs through it.

Okay, just off the top of my head because life is brief and real work beckons. Take out your copy (*Cien Años De Soledad*) and follow along. What follows is mine (with crucial differences sometimes italicized) and therefore what a just world would have received:

> Many years later, *in front of* the firing squad, Colonel Aureliano Buendia was to *recall* that *remote* afternoon in which his father took him to discover ice. Macondo was then a village of twenty adobe houses *constructed* on the edge of a river of *diaphanous* waters that flowed over a bed of *smooth* stones, white and enormous like prehistoric eggs.

The specific sounds of the letters, word order, relative incidence, line length, syntax; if you can preserve these and maintain fidelity to meaning shouldn't you? Moving on:

> The world was so recent that many things lacked names, and to *mention* them one had to point with a finger.

It was necessary to is so terrible here, though maybe not as bad as *in order to* just before it. If this was GGM's intent there were perfectly valid and expected Spanish equivalents. If you don't know them your Spanish isn't good enough, if you know them and ignore the above reasoning it's your English that's likely the problem.

Every year, in March, a family of *derelict* gypsies would *stake* its tent near the village and with a great *commotion* of *whistles* and bells display the latest inventions.

Stake, derelict, and *commotion* are just plain better; *whistles* just plain correct.

First they brought the magnet.

Hard to mess that up so no one did.

A *corpulent* gypsy with an unkempt beard and sparrow hands, who introduced himself as Melquiades, made a *truculent* public demonstration of what he himself called the eighth wonder of the *sage* alchemists of Macedonia.

Heavy and *bold* are so unjustifiable in light of the above options that I lose all faith in the endeavor. Yet somehow, like eyeballs to a gruesome car accident, I skip ahead past insufferable clunkiness and inartistry to:

In March the gypsies returned. This time they brought a telescope and a lens the size of a drum, which they exhibited as the latest discovery of the Jews of Amsterdam. They *sat* a gypsy woman at one end of the village and *installed* the telescope at the entrance to the tent. Upon payment of five reales, people *would* look through the telescope to see the woman within arm's reach. "Science has eliminated distance," proclaimed Melquiades. "Soon Man will be able to see what occurs anywhere on Earth without leaving his house."

Theirs is not terrible, unlike the following's equivalent:

One scorching midday they made an amazing demonstration with the gigantic lens: they placed a mound of hay in the middle of the street then set it ablaze by means of concentrated solar rays.

There is no reference to the sun in the original Spanish nor to any magnification hence none in the above translation and mound works nicely for *montón*, certainly better than pile. See how it works? *The sun's rays* here would be like *dry hay,* dumb. Later:

Jose Arcadio Buendia didn't even try to console her, entirely absorbed as he was in tactical lenticular experiments that he conducted with the abnegation of a scientist and even at risk to his own life. Trying to show the potential effects of the lens on enemy troops, he so exposed himself to concentrated solar rays that he suffered ulcerous burns that were slow to heal.

Fine, I added lenticular and arguably modified ulcer into its adjective form but said additions are yummy and amply supported by the record that is the original. Similarly, contrast this:

Despite the fact that trips to the capital were then only slightly less than impossible, Jose Arcadio Buendia promised that the moment the government placed its order he would attempt one so he could appear before the military powers-that-be to make practical demonstrations of his invention and personally train them in the complicated art of solar warfare.

With the gnarled mess the world got. It's all enough to make the non-Spanish speaking world jump ship before Buendia can even announce his discovery that the world is round like an orange.

In sum, can anyone prefer "an earthly condition that kept him involved in the small problems of daily life" to "a terrestrial condition that kept him entangled in the miniscule problems of quotidian life" and does preference even matter when the Spanish is *una condición terrestre que lo mantenía enredado en los minúsculos problemas de la vida cotidiana?*

Problematic English, finally then, is my diagnosis.

The invisible sounds they generate, sure, but also just the way some words look on a page, black ink on white paper, so that it almost seems as if even someone deprived of their sense would recognize their beauty:

LONESOME

Death is insufficient to us part, deaths are required.

. . . the literary equivalent of melody.

Art, or a purposeful form of play that seeks to illuminate Life.

The author's task is not to invent or even discover but to reassert, in compelling fashion, what we've long known to be true.

Melville dying in the gutter though he did damn near write The Gospels of his century.

. . . requires . . . special . . . selflessness . . . interest in others . . . inhabit . . . nature . . . engagement with . . . high . . . questions . . .

With proper Art man reminds himself of the ideal.

. . . great only insofar as it creates palpable human beings one can feel for; otherwise it's far more likely empty exercise designed principally to benefit the exerciser.

Perfection (v.) of which marks the zenith of human activity such that . . .

"Avenge me man."

"Avenge?"

"You mean avenge your death. His death he wants you should avenge."

"What does that even mean?"

"I'm dying bro, you see the blood."

"He's dying."

"No that part I get. It's the avenging part that stops me."

"Avenge my death."

"How?"

"How he says. Kill the man who killed him, there's no other how."

"Kill? I'm going to kill someone? From what I've seen society frowns upon that sort of thing."

"Society? Who brings up society at a time like this? It's his dying wish, just accede to it."

"Easy for you to say, I don't see you rushing to avenge. Go ahead. Take a blood oath to do so, there's plenty with which."

"That's silly, I don't know this guy from a hole in the wall."

"That's another thing. I mean I know you and all, but we were never really that close. Don't you have like a brother or something who can avenge?"

"Course not, don't you think you'd know if he had a brother? Falls on you man."

"My point exactly. If I don't even know if he has a brother, I'm probably not the best choice for avenger. I could probably be the guy who relays the message to his eight brothers that he wanted to be avenged."

"His death avenged."

"No brothers, avenge me. My death."

"What about, like, a really tough sister?"

"Will you stop? There's no time to lose. Look at him. Swear you'll avenge!"

"Fine, I'll avenge! But I don't even know where to start. Who's the recipient of my avengeance? Is that even a word?"

"Who did you man?"

"Also who asks for avenging? You own a deli, all of a sudden you're a goddamn Shaolin monk or something?"

"Know him?"

"No."

"Better describe him then."

"He's black."

"African-American."

"Great, I'm avenging a racist."

"Huge."

"Naturally, can't buy a break."

"What else? Nothing else, he's gone. You're going to have to run with that."

"Run? I can't even trot with that."

"You'll have to do some investigation. Start collecting fibers."

"Fibers?"

"Yeah, it all starts with fibers it seems."

"Fibers. You collect the damn fibers, you roped me into this thing. Fibers."

"Here's a fiber, a giant one. Yellow and spongy, what do you make of it?"

"That's a Twinkie."

Proper Art increases the recipient's capacity for empathy thereby increasing the world's store of Love.

Emily Dickinson's Letter to the World bound in a drawer away from any auction of the mind.

Ask the four if the forty come back no more and only the waves reply.

I am not a man who suffers fools gladly. In fact if you ever see me in the presence of a fool you will almost immediately note that I refuse to suffer him. Or if I do suffer him, do so in a manner that can never be mistaken for glad. Of course this inability and the biting comments it requires has earned me a well-deserved reputation, so that I will often hear my name come up in public discourse only to hear one party say something to the effect that *well you know he doesn't suffer fools gladly,* to which the other will respond something like *no, he doesn't.* Which reputation, of course, comes with its own responsibilities, so that many is the time I have found myself in the presence of a fool and thought *why don't you go ahead and suffer this guy for a while, where's the harm?* But then I'll remember what I'm known for doing with fools and I'll stop. Not that it's always easy to identify a fool either because many is the time that I've been going along suffering some person like it was the most natural thing in the world when I'll suddenly realize *hey this person's a fool, and what's worse I've been suffering him, gladly!*

... by filling it with allusive arcana for dimwit professors. Of course, he could've just written King Lear.

If the world is supported by a giant turtle what supports the turtle?

Don't be silly, it's turtle all the way down.

There's no void to fill, it's all void.

Blind Milton, penniless Melville, suicided Woolf and Hemingway, incarcerated Cervantes, epileptic Dostoyevsky, walking into a river your pockets full of stones, squeezing a shotgun between the floor and your forehead, wandering in the cold to your death, tuberculosis in the twentieth century right after a masterwork . . . but I concede nothing.

. . . an unhealthy fascination with technique and innovation to the detriment of the true and . . .

1. Narrative Poetry
2. Prose Fiction
3. Music

Just a cruel place, but one where the transcendental often walks alongside the cruel.

Character is foundational.

Art is a common language and commonalities combat loneliness.

Tis majority ruleth all.
The minor one, alone to fall.

The miner won a loan, two of all.
The mine or won, all own to fall.

The my nor won, a low an to a fall.
Them I know run, a lone two of awe.
Dumb I now run, all owe into Fall.
The my now are one, a loam too fall.

The My now are one
The mine are one
A loam too fall
I am one
All one
Too fall
A one
Alone

ONE

Because I no longer wish to be of you, I've tried it your way and it's empty, I don't want to monitor numbers or keep time like a metronome; I want the small part of life that flows through me to transmute then emerge as metaphor, clean and hard and inclusive but sharp enough to cleave the world that we the pained may digest it whole.

... to justify the ways of man to God.

The remainder is either truly indecipherable for a variety of reasons or else summarily deemed irrelevant to the relevant or even just excluded because inclusion would feel weirdly violative of something like Writer's privacy if that makes any sense.

IV

An Octogenarian Beginner Begins after Wondering if Beginner's Luck Even Applies

THE OCEAN [fn]

This is a stop at the beach, not a beach outing. Difference is with an outing Skye will collect the girls (four, six, eight) and everything they require and these appurtenances will be assembled near the door at the appointed time so that really his role will amount to nothing more exertive than going to the beach himself and, of course, before that, giving his terse imprimatur to Skye's idea of going to the beach *as a family*. So this is a mere stop and he is alone.

[fn]. The title of this work is derived in a singular manner. Although no title is written in Writer's hand, affirmative steps were seemingly taken to title the work as above. As indicated previously, the body of *The Ocean* was written in the margins of a ravaged TV GUIDE (one that displayed John Forsythe on its cover and wondered how long he could continue to resist various evil machinations). Said magazine always began by listing the reader's televisual options for the ensuing Saturday. Here, one of those options was a film called you guessed it and these two all-caps words are blatantly circled. The above story then follows and sorry if you disagree but *The Ocean* is its title. Regarding what may be objectors' primary objection, note that Writer displayed zero reticence about reusing others' titles as will be apparent to the discerning reader upon further development. Lastly, also singular is the film itself. Specifically, no other record exists of what is identified as this 1932 black and white motion picture and the people involved and I mean none; as in there is nothing you can click so don't bother and, yes, this is true in twenty-first century America. In short, it's as if it never happened. As if no *showgirl on the lam soon discovers the true depths of the sea's loathing of mankind.*

He is alone with Professor Stephen Tenrod, another way of saying Professor Tenrod is alone and a statement that is undeniably true and so because of a decision, really several decisions, made by the professor. And Tenrod is the kind who thinks the "p" in professor should always be uppercase even when not being used as appellation but because he does not herein control it isn't and won't. Back to the decisions, Professor Steven Tenrod decides to stop at the beach on his way home from the university because, well, truth is there is no prominent reason for this decision. Instead he finds that the luxury automobile slides effortlessly, as promised, from main highway to exit to somnolent side street of forgotten seaside village. Just as easily he finds that the vehicle orients not towards its popular areas but rather is inexplicably parking in the most desolate area of what is already a fairly desolate beach.

Consequently, when he removes his clothing and lays it on the damp sand there is no reason to take the universal therefore wholly ineffective precaution of wallet in shoe nor is there any problem with removing even the final sheer barrier that separates the clothed from the unclothed before entering the frigid water. And he is a distasteful task increment by increment type so this initial entry is followed by a pause and substantial exhale then ensuing steps become a demonstration of will until a partial eternity later he is in from the waist down with everything above dry as dust. From there, his body halved into pain and future pain, his hands suspended at varying levels, he is reduced to sensation and its immediate afterthoughts. The life of the mind extinguished by overflooded nerve endings.

He turns, submerging maybe another inch as a result, to look at clothes on a beach; the lumpy collection of fine garments he has placed on the sand, how they combine to form a layered mountain yet manage to retain individuated definition. So he is looking at that, taking slight backward steps, when really the first wave to register slaps his back to form a U of water around him and compel his hands into a hug. This is new pain and the body recoils from it. All the greater now that newly wet skin is beset by an insistent evil wind he had not heretofore sensed. The only solution then is to go ahead and sink up to his neck, his face the only segment still undisturbed by sea.

Now he sees that sun is reflecting off the face of his watch to form a focused line of light that reaches the one on his shaking body. The watch is on the clothes and the watch is expensive although he never really liked it until The Dean, who does like watches and therefore can speak of them intelligently, indicated without ambiguity that this specimen was tremendous; since that he loves the watch. To Skye he always loved the watch and its lyrical engraving referencing the constancy of Time even if inconstancy, in the final analysis, was really what surrounded the object.

Inconstant as in the way that, increasingly, Skye looked almost grievous, like something had been lost when far as he could tell it had been nothing but gain for years. Gain like when he became the youngest professor to attain the *distinguished* honorific at his university or the many others he subsequently researched. Or when their primary six bedroom was paid off and they were able to rather easily purchase the shore house currently responsible for his naked immersion in the vast ocean. Or how, most recently, he had accomplished what Skye seemed most fervent about and so, come fall, April would in fact be attending the prestigious Walstaff, he thinks, Academy. Again, these were clear gains yet each met with a barely perceptible but undeniable sense that a diminishment had occurred, and that's the loss that somehow registered on Skye's face until he began to maybe feel it too.

His clothes are the only thing on the beach. No, that's an over-simplification. There are other disturbances as well. There's been a contest on that beach. A Third Annual BallPark Frank Sand-Sculpture Contest has been held according to a banner on the distant maybe brown picket fence. The contest means people, twenty-first century people, have come and built complicated structures on sand despite presumably knowing what sand is and its futile relationship to the imminent water.

Sand, he knows, is essentially finely-degraded rock. Degraded by Life plus Time and if that formula can work *this* on *that* imagine it on the less sturdy. To build on sand is to deny all that in a deluded way. To build properly and for posterity use concrete. Concrete as in The Pantheon with its eighteen hundred years and counting. No less a personage than Brunelleschi saw that and largely followed suit to create art like *Il Duomo* that centuries later allows people like our professor to center their lives not on emulating him but on discussing exegetically what he produced.

No one will be discussing the sculpted sand in front of him but he now thinks he detects something like beauty emanating from there and so begins to make his way to the fragile creations that he may either confirm or dispel. In addition he sees that someone has unmistakably, using indentation, written on the sand and from his current angle it is impossible to discern the message. There's a message he feels. Someone has attempted communication in the strict sense of the word. The sand letters seek to extend up into their airspace and in that manner commune with their reader.

He wants to be that reader so the feet go up and forward, up and forward, and he gets closer he thinks but maybe not; in fact *definitely not* he realizes so he abandons walking and begins to swim in the exaggerated head swinging negatively manner of the merely competent swimmer. When he stops he has not covered a distance aptly commensurate with his effort and he is not big on physical effort so he decides to instead stay and stare until later doing what's required to reach shore.

The water is no longer cold although its temperature is unchanged. What has changed is the body in it, lowering to harmonize with nature. The sculptures he now feels he can do without but the writing is another matter. He longs to read it. He cannot from where he is stuck. He cannot ask anyone for help because there is no one who can help. He also sees now that the letters are enormous and numerous. What this means is that even when he later stands on the sand he may not, even then, be able to read the message from sandlevel. What he would need then is an aerial view.

How he sees it is that if there were a God and, further, you were He, you would look down and see emptiness interrupted but minimally. The competing sculptures, the clothes, and the writing that you would doubtlessly read. The only movement is water spilling over sand then hastily retreating, again and again. And this water is not travelogue aqua it is practically black and the sand white, meaning what you would see in constant repetition is Black encroaching on White, Dark on Light, Night on Day; Death, ultimately, on Life.

Maybe someone has the vantage point of God but none of his purported power. This someone looks down to see all and within this all is Tenrod immersed in kinetic water, his feet gripping unsteadily the sandy bottom. But the prospect of a flawed someone observing him unsettles the professor and makes him want principally to exit that water and clothe his body.

There is no such person he decides and as if in response the water moves him more palpably than before; pushes then pulls him, impels him forward before sucking him back in, closer to land then farther from it. Whether there is someone above, he supposes, is a form of speculation. That there is no other person in his visible vicinity is not, it is verifiable fact. He turns to look out at the water and sees the truth of what he already felt, there is no one out there either. Truth is, nothing is out there. There is no boat or craft of any kind, no buoys or other flotsam, no objects. Instead the water just flattens out as you move away from land until it forms, at a final distance, that paradigmatically sharp yet somehow still blurry line.

The line fills him with dread, always has. The seeming finality of the line undercut by its almost imperceptible curvature is maybe what does it. The enduring silence of infinite space is the phrase his mind quotes or misquotes when he sees that. It was a mistake. Everything that began with two hands moving the rounded apex of a wheel ever slightly to the right was mistaken and how terrible it then seemed to him that he was not Brunelleschi; that he did not build those structures, concrete structures that will endure as every living thing around them is erased.

It is no longer a question of desire he simply *must* decipher what is written on the sand. And it is not his imagination that he is farther from the writing than before. He tries to walk forward and finds he cannot. *Riptide* he says aloud and the sound of a human voice, even his own, piercing the silence troubles him. He is suddenly conscious of his breathing and unable to make it autonomic again. He must resume swimming only now he's tired. Fortunately, a wave rises up behind him just as he begins. It lifts and propels him and there is a moment where he feels weightless, supported and borne up by the very universe, ascendant in his safe return to solid footing.

But the moment passes, the wave that first lifted him now sluices under his body and continues on without him. He watches it reach sand as his feet touch down only to immediately slide back in rejection. He is still sensing his every breath and they are more plentiful than before. He is not a strong swimmer. *Riptide* he says again and tries to remember everything he knows about them. He's certain the solution involves the word perpendicular, or is it parallel? He often gets the two confused. Also horizontal and vertical. And when he needs to put something in alphabetical order he kind of still sings the song. He is naked in the ocean being taken deeper and thinking things like that.

He must rest. Gather his strength. If no one comes he will have to swim with great urgency to overcome the tensile water. It is water that has arrived here at long last from the remotest reaches of the globe and it now intends to flow back whence it came and begin anew the relentless cycle. The professor is no obstacle. He says all that aloud. He is floating on his back, drifting out and talking to empty air. He says the word riptide a few more times until it no longer seems to make sense; it can't be the right word, can't even be a word *period* its sounds are so funny.

Soon he will swim but is there a point if nobody comes? He calls for someone to come. If someone comes the whole thing becomes laughably easy but he knows no one will. He calls for someone to come. He is not yelling because he cannot. The sun is almost fully interred now. It will rise and fall, rise and fall, like a bouncing yellow ball and it will never stop. His shriveled skin looks simultaneously aged and fetal with a hint of subcutaneous water. The dying hair on his head is sporadic and matted down to its skull. The lips are blue. The water is not as flat out there as it looked from the sand and his body undulates up and down, so it takes strength to keep his face above water and it takes another kind of strength to keep thinking when thoughts no longer endure to completion.

The ocean is vast. What we call the world is just limitless ocean occasionally slowed by land and the people on it. The word *distinguished* is senseless too it seems. He is made in large part of water so water can't hurt him. If it happens what happens is you swallow and swallow until finally it laughs at your impotence and swallows you. The ocean is rocking him like an infant, bringing him closer then taking him farther. The closer water feels warmer. Each star in the sky contains the remains of a person once swallowed and their dolorous light would illume the earth even in our absence. There are more of yesterday's people in the water than today walk on land. The Halstaff, yes, Academy is no better than the second best academy. Someone will come if only he'll keep asking. He is closer and hears someone. He is farther and there is no one. He has not built anything, concrete or otherwise. There is something in the water. It floats. There is no moon. Anything holding it will float. Stars but no moon. He will reach it he sees. The watch will be back on his wrist, phone in his hand. He will call Skye, appeal to Skye. He moves purposely now, acting not acted upon. He is moving so he must be alive. The sky is never empty but below it often is. When he reaches it it is a shirt. It was always a shirt. It was always his shirt, swallowed by the water when the tide rose in reaction to the moon that wasn't there. The invisible moon was there all along, raising up the unceasing waters to cover the sand in forgetfulness and envelop his defenseless possessions. The writing, never read by a soul, has been obliterated; the sculptures have collapsed in on themselves. The shirt is there but it is nothing, it cannot help. It has a high thread count and Egypt is somehow involved. He lies back. He has to conserve energy until he swims. He will swim to shore. On his back he still moves, the water moves him. He is moving so he must be alive. His movement takes him closer then farther. Always the same. Closer then farther, closer then farther. Always. Closer. Farther. Again. The same. Closer then farther then less closer and farther still, less close then more far, less close than far, farther than closer, far farther. Then farther and farther and farther.

V

2nd of 3 Excerpts of Dr. Helen Tame's Introduction to Her Article: *Bach, Gould, and Aconspiratorial Silence*

Of this giant, orphaned at ten, ultimately blinded by life itself, who felt he was merely working but in truth made a gift to the world of immeasurable beauty, little need be said beyond a brief account of events he authored around 1741.

Around then, humans were still organizing themselves into things like Counts and one of them had trouble sleeping so had his Goldberg, fourteen but supremely gifted, play harpsichord (no pianos yet) for him in the antechamber in those instances, which playing must have set into stark relief the relative dearth of cosmos-rattling pieces existent at the time so that this Count Kaiserling sought out Bach to request a creation.

Bach's response was the following. A timeless aria followed by thirty variations thereof then a heartwounding repetition of the aria as if the whole of life hadn't just changed in the interim. The aria's melody is simple, if highly ornamented, but that's the equivalent of saying something like water is simple and so falls well short of the full story. Anyway, the variations do not spring from this melody but rather from its harmonic progression and they span the entirety of what can best be termed merely human experience.

Most importantly, it would take more than two centuries for the full significance of the above events to emerge. In those centuries Bach would die leaving his masterful *The Art of the Fugue* incomplete while other men would don uniforms that they might better enslave or liberate others with great improvement in the tools they used to do same, and while there's been a seeming decrease in man's ability to invent music like the variations the closer we get to today, there's also been an indisputable sea-change in our ability to preserve that music or more accurately performances of that music.

And somewhere in those centuries, on September 25, 1932 in fact—in a house in Toronto, Canada—to another family armed with Music, Glenn Herbert Gould was born.

VI

Players at Play on the Stage that Is the World

PERSONAE

List of Dramatic People

CLARISSA	A person
NESTOR	Another person
CHARLES	Yet another person
LUDWIG	A fourth person
LINDA	The same person
ADAM	The first person plural
NOT-ADAM	The last person singular

ACT ONE

A clinical but ambiguous room with five beds in the shape of an X. A terrible moaning by the four inhabitants growing in intensity and heartfelt pain until reaching a clamorous din. A gun is prominently displayed in a glass case in the corner below a sign indicating said gun is for emergency use only.

NESTOR	Wait a minute, I just realized I'm all moaning but not in any actual pain.
	(*all stop, seemingly coming to same realization*)
CLARISSA	Your point?
NESTOR	That this is bad enough without us having to create unnecessary noise, that point.
CLARISSA	So without physical pain no reason to moan, that what you're saying?
LUDWIG	(*moans loudly*)
NESTOR	What? (*at Ludwig*)
LUDWIG	You two aren't going to start up again are you?
CHARLES	Moans in agreement.
	(*Responsorial moans begin until eclipsing former intensity then suddenly they stop as the front of a wheelchair appears in the doorway. The occupant looks up at his pusher as to why they've stopped then gets suddenly and violently rolled forward until coming to rest at foot of Nestor's bed. Nestor looks down.*)
NESTOR	(*pointing*)
	Dear God look, his legs, they're hideously mangled, oh the horror!
WHEELBOUND STRANGER	They're fine actually. (*rising*)
LUDWIG	What's that you say? Call you Adam?
ADAM	I didn't say that.
LUDWIG	I know you didn't say *that,* you said call me Adam.
NESTOR	Yeah and why say *call me* all ambiguous-like. Your name Adam or not?
ADAM	It isn't and I never said it was!
CLARISSA	Relax Adam.

LUDWIG	Yeah relax, if you want us to call you Adam we will. We're easy that way.
ADAM	I don't, so please don't.
NESTOR	Easy, we all have names, I'm Nestor. Well, that is to say my name is Nestor.
CLARISSA	Electra, or Clarissa for short.
LUDWIG	Menelaus.
ADAM	Huh?
LUDWIG	Menelaus. M-E-N-E
ADAM	I know, but isn't anyone named Tom around here?
LUDWIG	Oh, Menelaus is just a nickname of sorts, it's not my real name, don't be ridiculous.
ADAM	What's your real name?
LUDWIG	Ludwig.
ADAM	(*blank stare at Ludwig then looking at now sleeping and loudly snoring old man hooked up to multitude of machines*) And him? His name?
NESTOR	It's actually funny you said that thing about any of us being named Tom. Funny in a coinciden-tal way I mean. An amazing coincidence really if you think about it. (*Others agree nonverbally.*)
ADAM	So his name's Tom?
NESTOR	Chuck, but you can call him Charles.
ADAM	So why, (*thinking better of it*) I'm just going to sit over here if that's okay.
CLARISSA	Suit yourself Tom, we were just moaning when you came in.
ADAM	I'm not Tom.

NESTOR	Of course not but your name *is* Tom and we *were* undoubtedly moaning when you came in.
ADAM	My name is most definitely not Tom, it's Adam. No (*angry at himself*) it's not Adam!
LUDWIG	Fine, but one thing you can't deny, Not-Adam, is that we were moaning when you came in and, furthermore, that moaning is undoubtedly contagious.
NOT-ADAM	My name is not Adam.
CLARISSA	Yeah, we heard you the first time.
NOT-ADAM	No, I'm making a negative statement here. I'm saying that when I tell you my name, which I will do shortly, that name will not be Adam.
NESTOR	(*slowly*) So why'd you say we should call you Adam with the aforementioned ambiguity?
NOT-ADAM	I didn't. (*frustrated*)
LUDWIG	There's a very simple way to end all this Not-Adam, one that I'm sure has occurred to you.
NOT-ADAM	Yes, of course.
LUDWIG	Simply tell us why you insist on being called Adam when that is not your duly-given, Christian name.
NOT-ADAM	No. (*more frustrated*)
CLARISSA	You refuse to tell us why the insistence?
NOT-ADAM	No, I'm saying that the way to end this is to tell you all my actual name. Which name is—
NESTOR	And to admit that we were moaning when you came in.
NOT-ADAM	Right. No! Moaning? What? (*No one responds.*) Anyway, my name is ... what moaning?
NESTOR	Which moaning.

NOT-ADAM	That's what I'm asking.
NESTOR	Which or what though?
NOT-ADAM	What?
NESTOR	Really? Because I lean to which.
NOT-ADAM	Huh?
NESTOR	No, huh-moaning makes no sense, I simply must draw the line there.
NOT-ADAM	What?
NESTOR	Fine, I concede and it's settled.
LUDWIG	How?
CLARISSA	When?
NESTOR	Where?
	(*Not-Adam is rapidly moving his gaze to each speaker.*)
CLARISSA	Why?
LUDWIG	When?
NESTOR	Said that already.
LUDWIG	When?
NESTOR	Before.
LUDWIG	Who?
CLARISSA	Me.
LUDWIG	Right.
NESTOR	Left.
CLARISSA	No, wrong. That right.
NOT-ADAM	Could we not talk for a while? I'll take this one. (*He takes the middle bed.*)
CLARISSA	To answer your earlier question, the moaning referred to went something like this. (*She demonstrates but the moans of ostensible pain soon take on a decidedly sexual aspect and as such the moans soon entrance the room's other inhabitants including Charles who sits up to get a better look.*)

NESTOR	So, Adam, welcome is what we're saying.
NOT-ADAM	(*not responding because staring at Clarissa*)
NESTOR	Adam?
NOT-ADAM	It's not ... (*frustrated then resigned*) fine. Thank you.
LUDWIG	Just him or all of us?
ADAM	(*puzzled*)
LUDWIG	Far as thanks go.
ADAM	Sorry, thank you *all* for the warm though luke welcome that has served only to add dis to someone who, for all his significant difficulties, was, on entrance, at least oriented and combobulated.
CLARISSA	Seriously we have far more crucial matters to attend to than the torturing of someone who's obviously easily disoriented.
ADAM	Easily?
CHARLES	And discombobulated.
LUDWIG	Oh, it speaks!
NESTOR	Goodness Chuck.
CHARLES	Charles for short, I insist.
NESTOR	We didn't take you for possessor of a functioning tongue.
LUDWIG	There's that *we* again, I'll thank you not to speak for us.
CLARISSA	And I'll thank you (*to Ludwig*) not to speak for us; perhaps we want him to speak for us.
NESTOR	Thank you.
CLARISSA	But we don't, I don't, don't speak for me.
LUDWIG	For me either.
NESTOR	So you guys thought Chuck, uh Charles, could speak ...

LUDWIG	No.
CLARISSA	Not in a million years.
NESTOR	… yet somehow chose to not utter a solitary syllable in the many months …
CLARISSA	Years.
LUDWIG	Decades.
NESTOR	… he's been here?
LUDWIG	He's an enigma.
CLARISSA	Enigmatic, a mystery.
LUDWIG	Mysterious, a riddle.
CLARISSA	Ridiculous, subject to ridicule.
CHARLES	I'm right here, I can hear you, and it hasn't been that long.
NESTOR	Wait, what do you mean by that?
CHARLES	I haven't been here that long, that meaning.
NESTOR	So how long?
CHARLES	Feels like I just got here really.
	(*Nestor looks at the others as if vindicated. They won't meet his eyes, except Adam who fails to see the relevance.*)
CLARISSA	You say *feels like* but you also recognize that you've been here a while, longer than any of us, right?
NESTOR	No, I've been here the longest.
CLARISSA	What are you talking about? I was here when you arrived. I remember it like it was yesterday.
LUDWIG	It *was* yesterday!
CLARISSA	That's right, it was. You just got here and already with the bossing everyone around.
NESTOR	I remember when Charlie arrived and it was a long time ago.
LUDWIG	Years.

CLARISSA	Eons.
NESTOR	Chuck has always been here and always will.
CHARLES	I'm leaving soon.
LUDWIG	No, he's never been here and never will.
CHARLES	I'm right here.
CLARISSA	Charles has never been where he's going and only gone where he's been.
	(*Everyone ponders that a while.*)
ADAM	But where?
LUDWIG	Who said that?
CLARISSA	The new guy.
NESTOR	New guy my ass, he's been here longer than any of us, even longer than Charles and Charles has never not been here.
CHARLES	He sure as Shinola was here when I arrived.
ADAM	Where when you arrived?
CHARLES	What?
LUDWIG	Who invited this guy?
ADAM	(*to Charles*) When you arrived where?
CHARLES	Here! What've we been talking about? (*looking to the others for support*) Believe this?
ADAM	But where is here?
LUDWIG	Right here (*gesturing*). See? (*all laugh*)
ADAM	But what is this? Where are we?
	(*Laughter stops abruptly and the ensuing silence is extended and palpably meaningful.*)
NESTOR	(*to Ludwig*) You were saying?
LUDWIG	I wasn't.
NESTOR	What?
LUDWIG	Saying.
NESTOR	What'd you say?
LUDWIG	I didn't say anything. You were saying *you were*

	saying and I was saying I wasn't saying. (*Pointing to Clarissa*) She was saying (*pause*) just saying.
NESTOR	Fine, (*at Clarissa*) you were?
CLARISSA	Saying? I was saying that when we say, say, what *was* I saying?
NESTOR	Exactly.
LUDWIG	Well that's settled then, off we go. (*No one moves.*)
CHARLES	Besides it's not where we are it's *what* we are and the answer is brains in a vat.
NESTOR	We debunked that already weren't you listening?
CHARLES	Listening as we debunked brains in a vat? No, missed that.
CLARISSA	Debunked is too strong, as I recall much spoke in its favor.
LUDWIG	Much indeed, great intuitive appeal.
CHARLES	Which one was brains in a vat again?
CLARISSA	Which one? How about the one you just declared the truth.
CHARLES	I know, and I remember being persuaded, just not very strong on the particulars right now, refresh please.
NESTOR	Brains in a vat, the thesis that we, the inhabitants of this room, are merely ...
CLARISSA	Certainly there was no definitive debunking.
LUDWIG	None.
ADAM	Of what? Where are we? Or, fine, *who* are we? Why? Are we.
CHARLES	We're brains in a vat.
NESTOR	That has not been established!
ADAM	The hell's a vat?
CHARLES	A vat is like a, you know, vat-like structure-

where, like, brains, mostly of a certain philosophical bent, are held and then ... what do I know I'm just a brain in a vat!

LUDWIG He's got you there.

CLARISSA You know those things called books Adam? It helps if you crack one open occasionally. Brains in a vat refers to the notion that while we believe ourselves to be corporeal beings moving through a physical world and experiencing heat, cold, pain ...

CHARLES Desolate loneliness.

CLARISSA ... in truth we are merely disembodied brains being stimulated in a manner that creates these illusions.

LUDWIG By an evil genius.

CLARISSA Not really a necessary component.

LUDWIG Who else would engage in such a stimulation?

CHARLES Is it me then, or is the evil genius making it a bit cold in here?

ALL It's you.

CHARLES It is me isn't it? After all this, the ups, the downs, the ins and outs, it's just me I'm left with and what I'm left with is not the greatest notion of who exactly it is I am.

ADAM Well, it was nice meeting you all but I'm afraid I'm going to be leaving now.

LUDWIG You should be afraid, that's the first thing you've said since you got here made any sense.

ADAM I'm leaving. Goodbye.
(*He doesn't move.*)

CLARISSA So long Adam.

CHARLES Sooo long.

NESTOR	Long enough, certainly.
ADAM	I'll stay … a bit longer I think.
	(The rest all look at each other, not the slightest bit surprised.)
CHARLES	Don't worry folks I remember who I am now.
LUDWIG	And the news is?
CHARLES	Good I think. When I was sixteen, at considerable risk to myself, I pulled a drowning child from a seriously turbulent river. I'm not even claiming it was selfless, but I so enjoyed the feeling that following the Marines I did swift water rescue for a dozen years until my body stopped letting me.
CLARISSA	Bodies will do that. You zig one way, they zag the other.
LUDWIG	Tyrannical is what they are.
CHARLES	Wait until you're dealing with one like this.
NESTOR	Never will. I plan to exhaust mine until it quits suddenly. There will be none of this … mechanical extension.
CLARISSA	That's good news Charles. Who you were, *are*.
CHARLES	I used to say that Nestor. I never wanted to be hooked up to this stuff. I used to talk tough man. Problem is the moment comes and it's hook up or check out. You know what? You hook up.
NESTOR	I find that when people tell me how I'm going to react to a given situation, they're invariably wrong.
CLARISSA	Never mind him Charles, you did the right thing hooking up.
NESTOR	Not when there's nothing can be done!
LUDWIG	What are you talking about? There's always

something can be done. There's respirators, ventilators . . .

CLARISSA   Refrigerators.

LUDWIG   Defibrillators, fibrillators as well obviously. Elevators, alligators . . .

CLARISSA   Incinerators.

ADAM   Impetuators.

NESTOR   Okay, that's not a word.

CHARLES   My wife, many years, used to say that she would die, I would die, but *we* would never die.

NESTOR   Why doesn't she say things like that anymore?

CHARLES   She died.

NESTOR   As will you, and as did the plural *you* at the time of your wife's.

LUDWIG   You don't know that.

NESTOR   Oh I don't?

LUDWIG   No, not *know.*

NESTOR   No?

CHARLES   The hardest thing at first was where I would do things like, without thinking, save some of the grapes I was eating for her. Because they were so good, or whatever, that you wanted that sensation of concurrent experience.

     Then I would remember and just leave them there to wrinkle out of flavor.

LUDWIG   A military hospital ICU Adam, to answer your question.

NESTOR   Where'd you get military from?

CLARISSA   Military's your objection? Where'd he get any of it from? Who says it's an ICU at all?

LUDWIG   You don't feel the care we're getting in this unit is intensive?

CLARISSA	Correct.
LUDWIG	Because I do. Hence the ICU.
NESTOR	Wrong, this an assisted living …
CHARLES	Dying.
NESTOR	… facility.
CLARISSA	In which no one is being assisted in any way? This is an insane asylum Adam. That's why you see so much disagreement. You can scarcely get sane people to agree on anything nowadays.
CHARLES	I agree.
LUDWIG	Me too.
NESTOR	I disagree.
CLARISSA	(*looking at Adam*) See?
CHARLES	Why do you care? Seriously, let's get down to it, why?
ADAM	Why do I care where I am? Doesn't seem a minor careless thing.
NESTOR	He speaks carefully, if anyone cares.
LUDWIG	Well then Adam, today's you're lucky day …
NESTOR	Night.
LUDWIG	… (*motioning with chin towards doorway*) because here's your answer.
	(*All look at doorway but there's nothing there. They look back at Ludwig, not understanding, then back at the entryway. Nothing.*)
CLARISSA	If this *were* an insane asylum wouldn't we, the insane, be the last to know?
NESTOR	Right, so your belief it is proves it isn't.
LUDWIG	Thought we agreed, more or less, on the vat.
CHARLES	*We* would never die she would say but I'm afraid it didn't prove so.
NESTOR	You're *afraid* it didn't or it didn't.

CHARLES   It didn't, and as a result I'm afraid.

CLARISSA   (*walking over to Charles and placing her hand on his shoulder*) I don't think there's any reason for fear Charles.

NESTOR   (*aside to audience*) I see ample reason, and little reason for anything else. And where none exists, I'll create.

CHARLES   We fear what we don't know and I fear we do so rightly.

LUDWIG   I fear nothing, and if anyone has less to fear than me it's you.

CHARLES   You mean *more* to fear than you.

LUDWIG   (*unsure*) Maybe.

CLARISSA   There's no reason for fear of any level, tell them Adam.

NESTOR   Don't answer that Adam, there just trying to scare you.

ADAM   I'm not scared at all.

NESTOR   Why do you think they're trying so hard?

CHARLES   I'm not scared either, thank you Clarissa. And I was wrong before when I said she'd died, that Linda had died. Linda wouldn't leave me like that, she'll be back. She said to wait here for her and that's what I intend to do. Her hand will be in mine again I just have to wait here. Placidly.

LUDWIG   Not sure this is the kind of place where you can just peacefully wait.

CLARISSA   Why not? The machines are working. You wait right here Charles. Your hand will envelop hers again.

NESTOR   Abandoned by your love, or let's just say by Love as an entity entire.

CHARLES   Love hasn't abandoned me … yet.

NESTOR   Because there is no love.

CHARLES   There is, I felt it before and I'll feel it again. I just have to wait here.

LUDWIG   Because out of even the bleakest darkness there must emerge a light.

CLARISSA   You wait right here baby, Love will be back.
             (*She walks away from Charles's bed and to Adam and Ludwig whom she addresses in a whisper.*)
             I'm worried about him, he has a distant look in his eyes I haven't seen before.

LUDWIG   On anyone?

CLARISSA   On … him … I guess, what's the difference?

LUDWIG   Want me to talk to him?

CLARISSA   Might be best.

ADAM   Excuse me, am I missing something? What good is talk going to do? He needs medical attention.

LUDWIG   You see all the machines, soulless blips and bleeps, what more do you want?

ADAM   I don't know, a *person?* Preferably one trained in medicine who would examine Charles and determine what, if any, salutary effect the machines are having and what adjustments should be made. Let's get someone like that in here.
             (*Ludwig and Clarissa look at each other but say nothing. Adam is awaiting a response but gets none. Instead, Ludwig and Clarissa sit resignedly on a nearby bed. In the meantime, Nestor has made his way over to Charles and sits near him so that only Charles can hear his words.*)

NESTOR   Comfortable Charles? (*Charles nods affirmatively*) Because I think I have to level with you. Now

SPRINGDALE PUBLIC LIBRARY
405 S. Pleasant
Springdale, AR 72764

I'm not a doctor, of course, but I've played one in various productions and I must say that I don't like what I see when I look at your charts. (*Charles looks around but, as he suspected, there are no charts in the vicinity*) You understand that as time draws to a close we either go out like docile lambs or we roar against it like lions. These are machines, heartless and cold, they can't help you when the moment comes. What comes into play then is your will. It's not coincidence it's called your last *will* and testament right? Your last moments are a testament to your will. What's yours Charles? (*silent pause*) You need to leave this room.

CHARLES   No, I'm to wait here for her return.

NESTOR   Whose return?

CHARLES   Uh ... she'll be back.

NESTOR   You don't remember her name do you?

CHARLES   (*confused*) Uh ...

NESTOR   Because it's lunacy to wait here for someone you don't know.

CHARLES   (*insulted*) I don't know my wife now?

NESTOR   She's certainly moved on by now, married someone else. There's only so much you can expect from a person.

CHARLES   No, she wouldn't do that. Wait here she said. She said wait here.

NESTOR   That's silly Charles. That's what they always say, don't you see?

CHARLES   No.

NESTOR   They say wait here, don't move, I'll be back. You know what the intent is?

CHARLES   To get me not to move?

NESTOR   Exactly, you don't find that suspicious?

CHARLES   She doesn't want me to move so that when she returns I'll be here and we'll be reunited.

NESTOR   Nonsense, you were never *united* in the first place. A proper union lasts forever and a truly eternal bond cannot be severed as easily as yours was.

CHARLES   There was nothing easy about it.

NESTOR   That's what you're dealing with here Charles. I'm surprised someone of your experience doesn't know better. Her lips moved and out came *wait here for me, don't move, I'll be back.* But what moved were the lips of a woman. Why do you think women's lips are so beautiful? To distract us from what escapes them, expelled by the serpentine tongue lying behind.

CHARLES   No, you don't know her.

NESTOR   I know *of* her. I know she's a woman, why else would you be so worked up? Ask yourself this. Who's been her biggest defender? Clarissa right? What a coincidence, the only woman here. They stick together man. Can you deny it?

CHARLES   I ... don't ...

NESTOR   Now, the sun shines on those who take action Charles. Stand in the dark and wait for harm and it will assuredly come.

CHARLES   *(shakes head slowly)*

NESTOR   But I'm sure you're right Charles, don't mind me. The things I'm saying are generalizations and as such they necessarily exclude *some* truth. You know the specifics well, making you well within your rights to tell me I'm mistaken and all is well.

CHARLES   You're mistaken, all is well.

NESTOR   See? I'm not upset to be mistaken. On the contrary, I've rarely been more relieved to be wrong. Feelings of insecurity are normal and don't necessarily portend anything untoward. The more I think of it the more certain I become that you're in the right Charles. You stay right here and wait, everything can still work out. And I'm going to be sitting right here, next to you, *every* step of the way. (*Nestor stands up and walks away*)
(*Nestor joins the others on the other side of the room. Adam has sat on the bed opposite Clarissa and Ludwig and he now moves over to make room for Nestor who sits next to him.*)

CLARISSA   We're trying to decide what to do.

NESTOR   What about?

LUDWIG   We haven't decided. That is to say, we've decided to *decide*, we just haven't decided the actual decision yet.

CLARISSA   What's he saying over there?

NESTOR   He wants to leave, I'm trying to talk him out of it.

CLARISSA   Thank you Nestor.

NESTOR   He says not to bring it up to him anymore.

ADAM   Why can't he leave?

LUDWIG   We're not saying he *can't* are we?

ADAM   Why shouldn't he then?

LUDWIG   Why didn't you leave when you said you were going to?

ADAM	I … changed my mind.
NESTOR	Yeah, if I had yours I'd try to change it too.
LUDWIG	We're in a safe place and once safety is achieved movement can only imperil that.
CLARISSA	This is not a safe place, we've had substantial evidence of that. This is a … strange place … where time seems to accelerate exponentially and the feel is of neither destination nor launch but rather of … stasis.
ADAM	What *do* we know?
LUDWIG	Or is it, what do *we* know?
NESTOR	I think it best now that Ludwig and I go on that investigation we were about to commence when we were so rudely interrupted by Adam.
CLARISSA	Yes, that might be best. Plus that will give Adam and me some time to catch up.
ADAM	Catch up? We just met.
CLARISSA	Exactly, think how much catching up that makes for.
LUDWIG	Remember that time Adam thought this was an insane asylum?
ADAM	I never …
NESTOR	That was hilarious.
LUDWIG	What a clown, way to project.
CLARISSA	Okay, so he was reaching. But the fact remains that unless one of us is willing to posit something compellingly plausible we're in no position to criticize. In other words, he gets points for trying.
ADAM	I didn't try. *You* said …
CLARISSA	Not a lot of points mind you but *points.* More than *we've* been able to accumulate at any rate.

LUDWIG	It *was* a good point when he said that if this were an insane asylum that would make us insane and therefore not really fit to recognize it as such.
ADAM	I didn't ... (giving up) thank you.
LUDWIG	You're welcome.
NESTOR	Welcome to stop throwing out wild conjectures that only serve to impede us in our search for truth.
LUDWIG	If your true and honest sole concern is that search, then why are you so resistant to what Adam is saying? That our failure to discover said truth is the strongest evidence extant that it simply doesn't exist.
ADAM	When did I say that?
LUDWIG	Not that truth exists but is somehow inapplicable to our present predicament but, rather, the greater inescapable conclusion that the larger concept being referred to simply doesn't exist. There is no truth.
CLARISSA	Now who's stretching?
NESTOR	Seriously, without truth what intelligent could we say about your just-concluded statement that it doesn't exist?
LUDWIG	You could intelligently say about it, and everything surrounding it, that it is meaningless.
ADAM	But would it be *true*?
NESTOR	Oh! The new guy contributes.
LUDWIG	Against all *odds*.
NESTOR	To draw *even*.
CLARISSA	A *prime* point, he's had a *number* of them.
NESTOR	Okay, that's enough.
CLARISSA	You're right. You two need to go on that inves-

tigation now. Only make it meticulous with an obsessive's attention to detail and an evident love of craft throughout.

NESTOR   Our investigation's over.

LUDWIG   Yes, we were heavily invested in it but like all human activity it came to an abrupt and violent end.

CLARISSA   And you found out what?

LUDWIG   We found nothing *out* but did find a lot that's in.

CLARISSA   In?

LUDWIG   Yes. At first we were inspired.

NESTOR   Intensely.

LUDWIG   Then incredibly, maybe inevitably, we were incited...

NESTOR   Inexorably.

LUDWIG   ... into the inescapable conclusion that inherent to our current incarceration is a certain indefatigable incoherence that intriguingly incorporates insufficient...

CLARISSA   Stop! You discovered what exactly?

LUDWIG   Nothing.

ADAM   Incarceration?

NESTOR   A profound epistemological failure.

ADAM   Incarceration?

CLARISSA   Doesn't sound like much of an investigation.

ADAM   Incarceration?!

LUDWIG   You okay Adam?

ADAM   Why would you refer to this as an incarceration?

LUDWIG   What would you call it?

ADAM   I call it... completely... voluntary... presence?

NESTOR   I agree.

ADAM	(*hopeful*) You agree that's what it is right?
NESTOR	Oh God no. I agree you call it that. And that's the important thing of course.
ADAM	No, that's not the important thing at all! What's important is what it actually *is*. Who cares what I call it?
LUDWIG	He has a point.
ADAM	See?
LUDWIG	I was referring to Nestor.
ADAM	Goodness. (*puts his face in his hands*)
CLARISSA	Can't believe you're still pushing that nonsense Nestor.
LUDWIG	He's only nominally pushing it. Nominalism.
CLARISSA	Well, I nominate Nestor for chief investigator of our predicament.
LUDWIG	I agree.
NESTOR	I disagree.
ADAM	I abstain.
CLARISSA	Of course the primary prerequisite for that position is the swearing of an ironclad, take-no-prisoners, vow of silence.
ADAM	Prisoners?
CLARISSA	Meaning we've collectively heard the last of Nestor and can safely proceed, without distraction, to a deeper understanding of this place and our role in it.
LUDWIG	Yes, it's a role!
NESTOR	But . . .
ALL:	(*immediately reminding him of his vow and silencing him with extreme prejudice*) Epp!

LUDWIG	A role! Don't you see?
CLARISSA	Yes, we have to roll with it. You're right Lud.
LUDWIG	Not saying that life is a certain way and we have to roll with it. Saying that what we call life is in fact *a role*. One we're compelled to play despite our distaste for the part solely out of a vague sense of loyalty to an outdated concept that dictates the show must go on.
ADAM	I don't understand.
LUDWIG	Explain it to him Clarissa.
CLARISSA	I will.
LUDWIG	Nestor and I now take our leave of you three and when we return we return armed with nothing less than a beautifully symmetrical and synergistically symbiotic explanation that will produce primarily anger at our failure to spot its blatant obviousness.
	(*Ludwig and Nestor leave, Nestor sticking to the vow of silence taken on his behalf. Clarissa and Adam remain seated near each other and apart from Charles.*)
ADAM	You're going to explain now?
CLARISSA	Explain what?
ADAM	If I knew, I wouldn't need you to explain would I?
CLARISSA	Now you're catching on, well done Adam.
ADAM	Where are we?
CLARISSA	Ah, you guys are all the same. Where are we, boo-hoo.
ADAM	Ludwig asked you to explain what he meant by that whole we're reluctantly playing a role thing and you said you would.

CLARISSA	I can explain.
ADAM	Good! Please do. What did he mean by roles?
CLARISSA	Oh no, I meant that I could explain why I told him I would explain.
ADAM	Oh god.
CLARISSA	You said it.
ADAM	Fine, explain that at least.
CLARISSA	Huh?
ADAM	Why did you say you would explain, when you had no intention of doing so?
CLARISSA	Well, I'd explain but it's highly complicated, and you wouldn't understand in a million years.
ADAM	Try me.
CLARISSA	I lied. Tell me Adam what's the long and short of it? Do you feel you've been here an extended or brief time?
ADAM	I . . .
CLARISSA	See? That's the problem, at least part of it. Another part is the sense you have that endemic to your presence here is an expectation that you will perform.
ADAM	How did you?
CLARISSA	And it's a mistaken impression on your part but it also pains me to inform you that your performance to this point has been anemic, so you're not really living up to this expectation that doesn't even exist and surely you see how problematic that is.
	(*Pause during which it appears Adam is considering Clarissa's statement but in reality is just the kind of silence that often emerges when two people who've been part of a group suddenly find themselves alone*

with little basis for speech.)

ADAM	So ... where you from?
CLARISSA	How would I know?

(silence)

ADAM	I'm from ... *(can't remember)*
CLARISSA	Never been.

(silence)

ADAM	You're right after all.
CLARISSA	Told you.
ADAM	All of you, right as rain. The *where* in *where are we* truly doesn't matter it's the how that counts. That's why we ask *how* are you on first encounter, the where is mere backdrop. I sometimes feel like a base animal where the only thing that matters is the immediate state of my senses. Hungry, full. Empty, sated.
CLARISSA	Deluded, alert.
ADAM	Pain, pleasure.
CLARISSA	So, Adam, are you pained or pleased?
ADAM	That's just it, as usual, fully neither.
CLARISSA	And yet, time doesn't wait for you to decide.
ADAM	No.
CLARISSA	It flows with merciless acceleration.
ADAM	But maybe let it, is what I'm saying. I'm not in pain, physical or otherwise. Truth is, this place is quite comfortable.

(Adam looks around in satisfaction as Clarissa shakes her head no, until his eyes land on Charles and he quickly averts them.)

CLARISSA	Humans adapt, and that's not a compliment. Unlike my older siblings, I was born into beauty. An elegantly constructed home in the shade of

one of those trees that seems to argue for the existence of God. As a child I was prone to behaving childlike and would earnestly say things like *I will never live anywhere else.*

But the tree grew sick and began to die, slowly. A century of prosperous life would have to ebb to an end in our presence. First one limb removed, then another, and now the house is too much in the sun to be warm and we notice that its owners don't smile in each other's presence and everyone's secluded in their own being, shedding limbs to protect the core.

That was the root of it, I remain sure of it to this day. Because the tree, like all that lives and grows, did die, and nothing grew thereafter. In the end, you grind up the stump and move away. A compartment shaded only by power lines. The girlish words have been emptied and you realize you'll live wherever the world damn well places you. That's where I'm from.

ADAM	That's not this, my circumstances before weren't any better.
CLARISSA	Through repetition, loss begins to feel like a transient curve.
ADAM	Maybe Nestor and Ludwig will discover something.
CLARISSA	That *may* be, maybe, but what if they only discover there's nothing to discover?
ADAM	Still be better than this … uncertainty … no?
CLARISSA	I'm not certain. Stop worrying will you? I promised you I'd get you out of here …
ADAM	When was that?

CLARISSA	… and I will.
ADAM	Wait a second, I'm the man here.
CLARISSA	If you say so.
ADAM	I should be the one promising everything's going to be okay.
CLARISSA	Go ahead.
ADAM	Everything's going to be okay. (*Clarissa cups her hand to her ear in expectation until Adam gets the message.*) I promise.
CLARISSA	Don't believe you. (*Adam deflates*) Understand, I'm not impugning your integrity, I just don't believe everything's going to be okay and you happen to be the one declaring the contrary.
ADAM	Just trying to stay positive.
CLARISSA	Positive?
ADAM	Yes, trying.
CLARISSA	No, I mean you positive that's what you were doing?
ADAM	Of course. If there's one thing I remain certain of …
CLARISSA	Let me stop you right there because if there's one thing *I'm* certain of it's that human beings don't often know what truly motivates their actions, agreed?
ADAM	I don't know.
CLARISSA	Exactly, you don't.
ADAM	No heaven or hell we don't ourselves construct is my overriding point Clarissa.
CLARISSA	Ah, there it is, right on schedule.
ADAM	You doubt it? Receive some tragic news and note how instantly the very environs you'd just drawn comfort from will transform into instru-

ments of the vilest torture. Note, contrarily, how a joyous enough development will free a man to kiss his severest enemy.

Are we to believe that all this—Life—is a mere question of geography? Locate yourself on the map so you know what to feel? I think rather we move through our world as if entering coloring book pages with only the barest outlines then start coloring.

CLARISSA   So now you've gone from base animal to supercilious artist freely creating his world? No wonder you're in no rush to leave this cocoon, little longer and it'll be a metamorphosed demigod filling this room with undergraduate-level musings instead of just you.

ADAM   I'm not hesitant to leave this room. I want to stay because I'm curious what will happen next.

CLARISSA   It's all very curious all right. Your every move beginning with that laughable pretense to disability. Very curious indeed.

ADAM   What, the wheelchair? I had no say in that.

CLARISSA   Did you say anything?

ADAM   No.

CLARISSA   Then you as good as essayed it. See what I'm saying?

ADAM   No.

CLARISSA   And don't think we haven't noticed what a turn for the worse Charles has taken since you arrived. Why should we forgive you for that?

ADAM   Forgive?

CLARISSA   No, why should we?

ADAM   I'm not asking for forgiveness.

CLARISSA	Good, cause you can forget it. We never forget, what for? Or give.
	(*Charles moans.*)
ADAM	I'm not responsible for that.
CLARISSA	If you're not able to respond who is? You're not suggesting...
ADAM	No one's *responsible*.
	(*They look at Charles.*)
	That there's the way of the world, he's ancient.
CLARISSA	Perhaps you're right. But O' how the ways of the world do seem to weigh on him now.
ADAM	As if the shell of his corpse can no longer contain the ghosts of everything he's seen and done.
CLARISSA	Do you feel guilty?
ADAM	I told you, I have nothing to do with...
CLARISSA	No, guilt at how much more vital you feel in his presence.
	(*Charles's breathing becomes audibly labored.*)
ADAM	Look at him. Maybe he once gave orders that men rushed to comply with. I bet he accumulated titles and positions, wrote his name in sundry registries that business might be conducted more expeditiously, but always with an eye towards the full and faithful credit of all his rights thereunder.
CLARISSA	I don't know, I rather think he toiled diligently at the secret arts. Repaid the niceness of a comely young woman with steadily increasing niceness until they became two halves of a whole with him maybe slightly less than half. From there it was just a long string of staying to the

	proper course through an incalculable number of imperceptible adjustments, the constant choosing of the right over the wrong.
ADAM	To what profit though? All his sums and take-aways culminate in a bottom line where his personal electricity no longer suffices and he has to plug his heart into an outlet if it's to keep pumping. What's he make now? What work product, and what does it earn him? What does he make of his various liens and levies now that the levee's burst and there's nothing left to lean on? A lifetime spent impersonating dignity and putting on airs but at the end nothing's too undignified provided it supplies the air needed to expend more life. Look at him gasping there. Living, no *dying* proof, at long last, that life is grand. Don't let anyone tell you different. Else why the white-knuckle grip on something that otherwise engenders so much bemoaning?
CLARISSA	I see proof all right. Proof that even a series of miseries, some so creative in their pestilence that even the cruelest soothsayer would decline to say them, is nevertheless preferable to what follows.
ADAM	I don't ...
CLARISSA	Besides, what we're saying is inapplicable to Charles. Charles is just going through a rough patch, not the end. Nestor and Ludwig will return with news and once so informed we'll get Charles the treatment he needs. Illness and wellness reside on the same side of the coin, it's just a question of giving that coin the proper

	flip. I want you to understand this point fully and memorably so I'm going to tell you a story.
ADAM	No thanks, just tell me the point.
CLARISSA	I'm going to, through the use of a story.
ADAM	That's just it. Don't want the story, just the point.
CLARISSA	What are you a savage? If I want you to know, really *know*, my parents were cheap growing up I don't just flat say they were cheap, do I? I say they treated nickels like manhole covers then tell you the *story* of how we had to bathe in the rain at our country house because they didn't want to pay extra for water. That's elemental.
ADAM	That's not cheap by the way, that's psychotic.
CLARISSA	So here's what happened. She was the kind of person who spoke to those closest to her primarily by making sure they overheard her remarks to others. The day we begin she had just returned from …
	(*Nestor and Ludwig are returning, we cannot hear Clarissa's story. Nestor addresses Ludwig outside the hearing of the others.*)
NESTOR	I sympathize with your human need to share, to enlist allies in a difficult spot, but I'm going to ask you to selflessly not share …
LUDWIG	You mean not selfishly share?
NESTOR	… and keep what we've discovered between ourselves.
LUDWIG	What have we discovered?
NESTOR	Yes that, keep it between ourselves.
LUDWIG	I don't *know* what we've discovered. I wouldn't even know how to begin to explain, other than

to say something like everything we thought was true is somehow neither true nor false and those things we deemed most irrelevant or its converse are not even susceptible to that kind of categorization.

NESTOR   Exactly, can you imagine the reaction?

LUDWIG   But.

NESTOR   You're our leader.

LUDWIG   Since when?

NESTOR   And leadership requires a certain kind of courage. What a person doesn't know is always more important than what he does know, and not just because it's orders of magnitude larger. Think of all you would unknow if you could, you know?

LUDWIG   No.

NESTOR   Exactly.

LUDWIG   They have a right to know.

NESTOR   You just said you don't know what you know, no?

LUDWIG   I know, but I also know they have a right to know what I don't know.

NESTOR   No.

LUDWIG   No?

NESTOR   No. They'll be looking to you more for a mood than any particular bit of information. Don't concern yourself so much with the content of what you say as with how you say it. This upcoming speech of yours will in large part determine...

LUDWIG   I'm giving a speech now?

NESTOR   ... how our friends view their predicament.

LUDWIG	Why would I give a speech?
NESTOR	Not why, how? And I'll tell you, summon your highest powers because the only thing this crowd respects is rhetorical excess.
LUDWIG	Not how, why?
NESTOR	Why, (*motioning with his chin toward Clarissa and Adam*) would you look at that?
LUDWIG	What?
NESTOR	Nothing. Couldn't have been more wrong I guess. Meaning when I repeatedly scoffed that love at first sight was as mythical as unicorns or virtuous women.
LUDWIG	What are you talking about?
NESTOR	About those two. I change my mind maybe once a decade but these two have me doing it hourly.
LUDWIG	Change how?
NESTOR	Well surely you saw what passed between them at respective first glance. So palpable that I began to reconsider my position. But then, when nothing seemed to germinate from there, I remembered how you and Clarissa had shared something similar on your first meeting.
LUDWIG	Not true.
NESTOR	And so concluded that calling these admittedly charged interactions Love was highly presumptuous, at best, and I was safe in my earlier position. But now, see for yourself. What they're obviously experiencing now *was* apparently evident from their outset. So there you have it. Against all impediments, love at first sight. A glimpse into the future of a two always meant to be one.

LUDWIG	Good for them I guess.
NESTOR	Of course …
LUDWIG	What?
NESTOR	Well, only that if I'm right about what previously passed between you two.
LUDWIG	You're not.
NESTOR	Then it seems what we're seeing is more like happy happenstance, happy for them anyway. Ironic too.
LUDWIG	If you say so.
NESTOR	Adam convinces you to risk your life and leave them for the benefit of the group and your absence just happens to open the door to their obvious connection.
LUDWIG	You mean *our* absence.
NESTOR	Obviously, if the roles had been reversed or, I would argue, even if they were to reverse now and Adam were to absent himself, that could easily be you in the breathless throes of love.
LUDWIG	I'd rather breathe.
NESTOR	Of course, (*solicitous*) I didn't mean to suggest otherwise. Just that … this can be a lonely place. Charles has what's left in his neurons of Linda. Clarissa and Adam now have each other. I *guess* you could argue that the spare tire's just as important as the four that spin.
LUDWIG	What does that make you?
NESTOR	I drive, else I get dizzy from the lack of control.
LUDWIG	I'll be all right Nestor, but thanks for the concern.
	(*Clarissa notices them.*)
CLARISSA	Guys! You're back! What news if any?

(*Ludwig looks at Nestor who smiles but doesn't respond.*)

CLARISSA   Well?

LUDWIG   Um...

CLARISSA   Nestor?

(*He doesn't respond so Clarissa looks to Ludwig.*)
What's with him?

LUDWIG   Oh, probably that vow of silence you made him take.

CLARISSA   Goodness. Fine, you can disavow your silence. Now, what happened?

(*Nestor crosses his arms and ruefully indicates no in a manner consistent with his vow. Adam and even Charles, to the extent possible, have joined Clarissa in hopeful expectation.*)

LUDWIG   I don't think he's going to spill it.

CLARISSA   You then, what did you find?

LUDWIG   Well (*hesitant*) it's not easy to explain.

(*Nestor hits him on shoulder.*)
But I will say this: (*clears his throat*) the trajectory of human progress has rarely if ever formed a straight line.

(*Their interest is piqued.*)
If, as some suspect, we are what's left of humanity, then nothing short of cosmological propulsion has landed this burden on our lap. History will record our reaction, but more crucial than that, our reaction will determine history. Not just its content but whether such an entity will even endure.

At issue is what will become of this grand edifice. We built it up and into the sky in the hopes of reaching heaven and now as it crumbles down around us we find that this great distance we thought we'd traveled can close in an instant. So what now? Because a person flung backward by adversity can run away in the direction he was flung, stay put, or slowly, grudgingly, inch-by- inch until foot-by-foot begin the journey back whence she came to resume the struggle.

I won't pretend that what Nestor and I learned is encouraging in the classic sense, he loves and respects you all too much for that, but it does have the power to encourage in this respect. In the agency of Man lies his majesty. What will become of us is largely a function of us. I urge you to take action as it is only in acting that the actor becomes fully human. A second act is guaranteed no one and in this respect it is often the lone individual, not the nebulous group, who must stand firm as a host of tragic natural and other forces array against her.

So we concede that we may not have secured satisfactory answers, but we did succeed in narrowing what was an infinite universe of possibilia into primary and irreducible questions.

What is a question anyway? That's my question. Why do we question, that is the true question. Why not content ourselves with what we know, which is considerable, and leave undisturbed the great sea of the unknown? Damn, the word quest is built right into the evil thing.

Who should go? How soon? Is their success

and glory as assured as it seems? Why can't we all go? Why does one person get all the good fortune and why is it so urgent that they leave as soon as possible? They're you have it. Now let's answer.

ADAM   The hell's he talking about?

CHARLES   And who the hell suspects we're all that's left?

NESTOR   I think he's saying it's up to Adam, all our hopes rest on him.

CLARISSA   What happened to your vow?

NESTOR   Translating doesn't count, you know that. More importantly, the man makes a lot of sense. Are we to believe that Adam's late arrival, with that name, is mere coincidence? He was formed out of dust to save us and the time is undoubtedly now.

LUDWIG   Actually, I was thinking Clarissa.
(*Nestor looks at Ludwig with genuine surprise.*)

CLARISSA   Thinking me for what?

LUDWIG   For our hero, or I suppose heroine.

ADAM   No way, it's too dangerous. Nestor's right, I should be the one to go.

LUDWIG   What's required here really is a woman's touch Adam. I'm only thinking of what's optimal.

CLARISSA   I'll go, no problem, but I do want to know what that entails.

NESTOR   Maybe you're both right. Clarissa can go and be the primary, but Adam will escort her for protection.

LUDWIG   No! I mean ... I think it's clear that this ... is a one-man, uh woman ... job's what I'm saying.

CLARISSA   Protection? I think having to worry about pro-

	tecting Adam would just get in my way.
ADAM	I think he meant I would do the protecting.
CLARISSA	But what's the job exactly? How about we start there?
NESTOR	The job was and is ever thus: to shed restrictions and rise.
CLARISSA	Less lyricism and more clumsy exposition please, the sun is sinking.
NESTOR	Very well, it appears we've found a way out. Those of you familiar with this place will from experience understand the key use of the word *appears*.
ADAM	So let's go, what are we waiting for?
CLARISSA	No, I understand, I have to go alone. I'll gather my things and maybe prepare some closing remarks.
ADAM	You mean departing remarks.
CLARISSA	Yeah, what you said.
	(*She leaves.*)
ADAM	I'm at a total loss here.
NESTOR	(*aside*) Would that were true; you haven't yet begun to lose.
ADAM	Can someone please explain to me what is happening?
NESTOR	I believe someone has been looking for just that opportunity. Someone, I mean Ludwig?
	(*Ludwig and Adam move in the general direction of Clarissa, leaving Nestor to sit next to Charles.*)
NESTOR	I hope you're not too upset Charles. I certainly argued on your behalf but this democracy thing's a real bitch huh?
CHARLES	Whatever are you talking about?

NESTOR   You know, about who gets to go. The fairer sex
and all that, though if you ask me there hasn't
been anything fair about sex from the get. I
mean, you see the way those two look at her,
and of course there was never any question
which way she herself would vote.

I must confess I took my oratorical skills for
greater than they proved. After all, I persist in
my belief that the merits were on our side and if
a truly gifted rhetorician should succeed quite
independent of his position's inherent vice or
virtue what do we make of my failure to convince on behalf of the meritorious side?

Honor thy aged until they cease to age, that's
how I was raised. So, obviously, when it came
time to decide who gets to go, I immediately
lowered my lever for you. Problem is Clarissa
was seemingly able to win Ludwig and Adam
back to her side by raising their levers.

It's a common misconception and those two
are nothing if not common. If y'aint got nothing, you got nothing to lose, and therefore if
you have little, in your case little of what we'll
call future life, you by extension have little to
lose. Of course, you and I know different.

The reason the widow giving alms is so im-
pressive is because it's infinitely harder to part
with what's scarce right? Anyone can watch
their surfeit dwindle slightly but try and wrest
that last piece of bread from the street urchin
and see where that gets you. By that analysis, if
staying in this room is an invitation to Death, as

seems clear, then it's actually you who has the most to lose.

You who've witnessed the unspooling of a long, rich life. Who've tasted every possible permutation of the bitter and the sweet. Only you among us truly understands what all can be lost.

So I argued and so was I overruled by my insensate audience. There are some who would argue a form of civil disobedience at this point. Alas, I cannot bring myself to say what reflexively forms on my tongue, that you may rightly controvert an authority derived solely from numbers in a matter of such importance.

The good news, I suppose, is that if you mindlessly accede to their decision you won't live to regret it. I mean you won't have the sensation of realizing you were wrong if you stay, so the decision to stay would be senseless in a sense. Either way, don't blame them Charles, they're just kids.

(*Charles sits up but says nothing. Nearby, Ludwig is done informing Adam and moves toward Clarissa, who is preparing to leave, before pausing to think out loud.*)

LUDWIG Damn me if the mere voicing of questions hasn't led me to *question*, resulting in an ever-expanding universe of explananda. And send me further down if that's not the way of this place, where what we say with conviction determines truth more than the other way around. Yet this remains a time and place to act *on* not *in*.

(Ludwig turns and returns to Adam. Clarissa remains alone preparing.)

CLARISSA And precisely when does an eager embrace with Death's most trusted deputy convert into a kind of plausibly deniable self-immolation? Who wears more blame? He who sits on the piano to play poorly or she who ignores the strident notes and allows herself to be played on?

Maybe I'm more like a player piano, feed the sheet and listen to the highly predictable result. If so I aver that I'm out of tune. I can sound the notes, vary their volume and timbre, but they'll no longer take melodious form.

At least if unjust suffering is somehow graver I can content myself with the justice of mine. After all, should I not feed on the same meal I prepared and served others? And if I consume more of it and accordingly get sicker is that not just?

(Ludwig enters.)

LUDWIG You know, Clarissa, I didn't mean to suggest that you had to be the one to go.

CLARISSA I'm sorry, you were mean to suggest what?

LUDWIG No, I'm saying I didn't *intend* ... to insinuate that ...

CLARISSA Don't worry Ludwig, I think I understand.

LUDWIG You do?

CLARISSA Of course, you feel guilty.

LUDWIG Guilty?

CLARISSA Sure, I know what you did.

LUDWIG You do? I can explain.

CLARISSA	I mean, you had this great benefit to confer and four friends in great need of beneficence, and you essentially chose me. Don't think I don't appreciate it is what I'm saying.
LUDWIG	Listen.
CLARISSA	So grateful am I, in fact, that I'm going to *ex post facto* make you feel better about your decision.
LUDWIG	Listen.
CLARISSA	Because I haven't told anybody this. But I have a child, a son, I'll be returning to.
LUDWIG	A son?
CLARISSA	Yes, a star so powerful his rising and setting is momentous enough to determines my days. And here's a thing rarely voiced about the parent-child dynamic. Someone, let's say an infant, is born. An adult, maybe two, will then fix its gaze on the reluctant arriviste and experience an emotion so strong we had to name it love. The possible commonplace is that said adult's love for the child will continue to grow throughout the child's lifetime, despite the indubitable fact that the recipient becomes less loveable over time. Any doubters can witness the inevitable mother's background tears as her reprobate son is led to the electric chair.

The ugly secret, of course, is that the child's love for the adult will not grow. It will dwindle and fade commensurate with Nature's assault on the relevant body. Now, this lack of reciprocity may ensure an orderly revolution between the living and the dead, but it can be a cruel turn for those who end up at the bottom, longingly eyeing their former perch.

LUDWIG I didn't know. When I said you should be the one to go ... I ... didn't know.

CLARISSA I know, but now it's all the more perfect. Let's go, (*gathering her things*) I've prepared some words.

(*Clarissa leaves suddenly, moving toward the others and leaving Ludwig alone.*)

LUDWIG Do I even have to say that someone had to go and that this someone will inevitably have built human connections they must jeopardize? It would have to be the strongest connection we know of though: a mother and her son, a son folded into his mother. Isn't an offense directed at her most powerful emblem a blow against Life itself? And wouldn't banishment then constitute an appropriate retaliatory deprivation?

No matter, because the equities cry out in my favor. Did I not feel my breast swell with truth as I declared that someone had to go? And didn't that swelling subside only slightly when I identified her as the ideal goer? I say true words animated by false air retain their value as truth and a proper end justifies my meaning. That then settles the matter.

(*pause*)

Yes, quite the settlement. Any doubt as to guilt rejected as not reasonable. For, like a cough in the fugitive dark, the rationalization identifies and exposes the guilty. Lady and Gentleman Factfinder: he sought to rationalize his actions through florid speech and The Judge will instruct you that you may properly infer a consciousness of guilt from such a flight away from truth.

(*pause*)

But there remains time for the remedy to halt any poisonous progress!

(*He runs toward Clarissa to find her standing with her belongings near the exit and formally addressing the others.*)

CLARISSA In sum, I think the coinage *heavy heart* caught on more out of alliterative allure than any great metaphorical value, so I'm striving here for a more genuine and revelatory ...

LUDWIG I'm sorry to interrupt, Clarissa.

CLARISSA Yes, you are.

LUDWIG But could I have a word with you?

CLARISSA You can have as many as you want provided you don't take them from me.

LUDWIG (*looking at the others*) Has to be a private word guys.

NESTOR Well if that doesn't beat all. Privacy he says, as he makes a public spectacle of himself. Well, never mind, Charles knows when he's been insulted. Let's go gentlemen.

(*They don't move but instead draw closer that they may better hear. Finally, Clarissa and Ludwig move away.*)

CLARISSA What is it? I was just getting rolling.

LUDWIG I feel I was maybe slightly less than straight with you but in my defense ... um ... I wasn't honest before.

CLARISSA That's some defense.

LUDWIG	When I said you should be the one to go and painted a rosy picture of what you could expect, when I did that I was lying.
CLARISSA	I see, paint for me a more accurate picture then.
LUDWIG	It's not good. The picture's not altogether clear, but through the snow and other interference what I see is problematic.
CLARISSA	You say what *you* see, but wasn't Nestor at your side? Did he not see the same as you?
LUDWIG	How sure can we ever be of what another has seen or experienced? But I believe he saw the same.
CLARISSA	I see.
LUDWIG	I'm sorry, it's with a heavy heart that I . . .
CLARISSA	Stop! I want for motivation, not apologies.
LUDWIG	But you're right to lack motivation, you shouldn't go.
CLARISSA	Not my motivation, Ludwig, yours.
LUDWIG	Oh.
CLARISSA	And?
LUDWIG	Just . . . the thought of being alone . . . eternally . . . not joining with the opposable sex . . . Nestor made some good points . . .
CLARISSA	Ah.
LUDWIG	. . . about the advisability or romantic love and such.
CLARISSA	Say no more, preferably ever.
	On subsequent thought, tell me, what *is* unrequited love like? I've never experienced it, at least not from the end you're in. Oh, and sorry I couldn't requite.
LUDWIG	No, you don't understand.

CLARISSA	I just admitted as much. I simply can't conceive of demonstrating love towards someone to no effect. Although I must say that your demonstrations lacked the appropriate vigor, not that any amount of vigor could have overcome the nullity that is my inclinations towards you. Silly boy...
LUDWIG	That's just it.
CLARISSA	... all you needed was a one word explanation: jealousy. I can scarcely think of a more valid human emotion.
LUDWIG	Jealous, yes, but not the way you think. Not jealous of you, but of him.
CLARISSA	Precisely.
LUDWIG	Wait, how does that work? Who are you jealous *of* when you wish...
CLARISSA	Listen, I'd love to stay here and hash this out with you Mr. Full-of-Surprises but time matters here and I have to get going. Yes, I'm still going. As for your conscience, you can let it rest in peace as it's nothing you said impels me. The next person to embark on a successful manipulation of me will be on a maiden voyage.
LUDWIG	You knew? Then why...
	(*Clarissa leaves abruptly towards the exit and after a moment Ludwig follows urgently. There they find Charles in the process of hobbling out.*)
ADAM	Clarissa quick!
NESTOR	He insisted, insistently.
CLARISSA	What's this now?
CHARLES	I'm going. I need to be the one who goes and there's no time for debate.

CLARISSA	There's always time to listen to reason right Charles?
CHARLES	You want reason? I have all the reason I need. The reason I'm going is that, unlike you all, I do not have the luxury of time to wait and see how it all works out in the end. My end nears and I need to work against it.
CLARISSA	Just listen, Charles, because we have strong reason to believe that what you'll find out there will not be great.
CHARLES	So who do you say should go?
CLARISSA	I'll go, like we decided. (*Charles and Nestor exchange a quick glance*) If everything's fine I'll come back for the rest. If not, you'll be safe here.
CHARLES	I'm not safe here, I'm not getting better.
CLARISSA	Maybe not, but you're also not getting appreciably worse. I'll come back if everything's fine.
CHARLES	No you won't, why would you? Linda said she would return and the only thing that replaced her was desolation. She said we would never part.
CLARISSA	She was using metaphor Charles.
LUDWIG	A perfectly legitimate way to speak.
CLARISSA	You know that.
CHARLES	I'm going, I have the most to lose. (*He resumes hobbling.*)
LUDWIG	Wait! (*Ludwig removes his hat and beautiful long hair unfurls. He removes his jacket to reveal that he is a woman, a striking one! Adam and Clarissa look at each other, Nestor doesn't react. Charles moves closer to get a better look.*)

CHARLES	Heaven!
LINDA	See, it's me, it's Linda. I told you I'd return and I did. We're together again, don't leave.
CHARLES	Linda?
LINDA	Yes, Linda. Stay.
CHARLES	Say my name, say my name Linda.
LINDA	What?
CHARLES	Say my name. The first time I heard you say it the sound fluttered my heart, and though the effect did dim over time it remained perceptible to the end.
LINDA	There was no end, it's me.
CHARLES	Say it then!
LINDA	There was no end Charles.
CHARLES	(*upset*) Oh. No. Say it. Say it please.
LINDA	I just did Charles.
CHARLES	Oh. (*looks away then up*) What did we call soft displays of affection?
LINDA	What?
CHARLES	What did we name them, it's a simple question.
LINDA	I don't ... know.
CHARLES	A photograph. A remarkable photographic likeness but developed in Hell not Heaven. Tell me, if left in the sun will you fade and desaturate? (*He hobbles off.*)
LINDA	This is a confusing place, give me a moment.
CHARLES	I don't have one to give. Chubby, we called it chubby. (*He leaves.*)
LINDA	Wait! You're right! Charles! (*The four stand dumbfounded. Charles is gone. Sud-*

denly Adam draws a sword heretofore unseen and puts it to Linda.)

ADAM Who are you? Speak!

CLARISSA Where the hell did he get that?

LINDA I'm outspoken, I've spoke all I will. If you want more verbiage you'll have to provide it yourself.

ADAM I'm not playing! *(pushing sword closer)*

NESTOR Easy Adam, *(taking the sword and throwing it offstage)* silence is always a woman's prerogative. Right Lud old boy?

CLARISSA Wait! Do you guys hear that?
(Soft and vague human sounds are heard.)
Those are muted squeals of delight, Charles is in a better place!

ADAM No, I think they're cries for help.
(more sounds)

CLARISSA No, I tell you. Can't you divine the meaning of those sounds? We are in a safe place, protected by a benevolent deity, partaking of splendid riches of florabundant variety and an enriching power that offers powerful enrichment.
(As Clarissa speaks a ball rolls in from where Charles left. Clarissa stops as Linda approaches it to investigate. She goes closer and closer until making the wretched discovery that it is Charles's head! What was his head. She unloads a grievous scream and recoils in abject horror. Adam and Clarissa are so stunned their horrified grief is displayed as if underwater.)

CLARISSA Oh my . . .

ADAM God.

*(Nestor calmly removes his jacket, wraps it around
his elbow, and goes over to the case, where he smashes
the glass with it and removes the gun.)*

ACT TWO

The same room, but different. In fact, nothing in it is the same as
before. At a small round table sit Adam and Linda in a seeming
portrait of placid domesticity. The beds are gone and in their
place, near the exit, a stack of sandbags.

ADAM	Wait, what are you saying exactly? No equivocation please.
LINDA	I'm saying behave like an adult. Change fuels the world and powers the globe's rotation. Leaves lose their grip on the tree that provided them sanctuary to then brown and curl on the ground. But their decomposition feeds the soil that greater splendor might grow thereon.
ADAM	That's your version of unequivocal?
LINDA	I'm sorry, did I promise you a lifetime?
ADAM	Yes! Precisely that!
LINDA	I may not have realized at the time how precious a commodity that is.
ADAM	I'd respect you so much more if you'd just come out and say it.
LINDA	Well, Adam, if that's your real name, I'm afraid this may seem premature, but I don't think this is working out.
ADAM	Premature? We've been together decades!

LINDA	Does seem that way at times doesn't it? I'm sure you understand.
ADAM	I most definitely do not! Is it another man?
LINDA	No.
ADAM	Then?
LINDA	Another woman.
ADAM	*What?*
LINDA	I was another woman when I declared that life-time thing. Such another, in fact, that I'm only taking your word for said declaration.
ADAM	That's outrageous.
LINDA	Understand, what we call a person is just a product of their particular genetic stew and how those ingredients are basted and braised by the specific experiential heat burning in its kitchen. Do I not get to produce different flavors as those flames of experience vary?
	You would bind me through the words of my priors, but I state honestly that you might as well seek to use the disembodied words of a radio announcer for all the connection I feel to them. Is it solace then to say that I have not fallen out of love with you but rather that this *I* never loved you at all?
ADAM	No, it's not, not even close.
LINDA	I say with confidence that what is needed for this type of thing to work is a derogation of sorts and one that I suspect I'm not really capable of.
ADAM	No, not true. It's an enhancement what we did. A doubling of skills and assets.

LINDA	Tears and tirades.
ADAM	You're purposely taking a myopic view.
LINDA	No, on this I'm 20/20.
ADAM	So that's it then?
LINDA	You don't have to say it like that.
ADAM	How do you want me to say it?
LINDA	(*cheery*) So that's it then!
ADAM	I think you're mentally ill.
LINDA	Thought's crossed my mind. But maybe true insanity resides in thinking that an artificial social construct is going to fill a void that's not societal in nature.
ADAM	Love is not a construct.
LINDA	Love, Adam? At this late a stage?
ADAM	Yes, Love. You have something better?
LINDA	Yes, our daily bread. Because I can see it, it weighs down my hand and fills my stomach.
ADAM	But then the emptiness returns.
LINDA	Which is why I need a constant supply.
ADAM	It can't fill that void.
LINDA	Maybe not, but I'm wise and don't expect it to so there's none of that unbearable disappointment.
ADAM	There's no talking to you.
LINDA	Promise?
ADAM	Don't talk tough, you'd regret it.
LINDA	Let's see.
ADAM	Fine.
LINDA	We're going to see?
	(*histrionic silence in response*)
	Great, let's see.
	(*Clarissa and Nestor approach speaking only to each other.*)

NESTOR	You trust her?
CLARISSA	Does that question presume, Nestor, that I trust you?
NESTOR	Not at all, we'll get to me, what of her?
CLARISSA	You mean the her we thought was a him?
NESTOR	The very.
CLARISSA	You're asking if I trust someone who lied about the most fundamental aspect of their humanity?
NESTOR	She explained that.
CLARISSA	That, right.
NESTOR	What?
CLARISSA	You found that explanation persuasive did you?
NESTOR	Why? You didn't? What part?
CLARISSA	Where to begin? Let me see if I got it all because it's been a while. She *is* Linda, that is, her name is Linda. But she's not the Linda who Charles filled our ears about. Only, she was able to fool Charles a bit because she looks just like that Linda because *that* Linda is *our* Linda's twin sister. That's right, the Lindas' parents didn't just have twins and presumably dress them the same, they took it a step further and gave the two girls the same name!
NESTOR	Where's the problem?
CLARISSA	Only they're then separated at birth, live semi-full lives on different continents during which they remain aware of each other's existence but learn to accept the absence of any real relationship until finally our Linda decides she will make contact, only the ship she's on becomes shipwrecked leaving her here, where she inexplicably decides to pretend to be Ludwig that

she might better investigate certain matters that really didn't need investigating. And there was something in there about royal blood as well, as I recall.

NESTOR   Again, where's the problem?

CLARISSA   Doesn't seem farfetched to you?

NESTOR   No. Well, maybe medium-fetched, but far? Nah, far?

(*Linda and Adam approach.*)

CLARISSA   Okay, never mind, not a word.

NESTOR   Clarissa suspects your backstory, Linda.

LINDA   Suspects it of what?

NESTOR   Of not being true I suppose.

LINDA   Really?

CLARISSA   Well …

ADAM   Linda admitted as much to me but swore me to secrecy. She seemed especially concerned that Clarissa not find out.

CLARISSA   Is that right?

LINDA   Adam agreed but argued that the real person to mistrust was Nestor.

NESTOR   I see. Was that before or after you confided in me that you were thinking of ending you and Adam?

ADAM   You confided in *him?*

LINDA   Why not? After all, he is a confidence man.

ADAM   After what he did to …

NESTOR   Who?

CLARISSA   Charles.

(*At mention of the name all grow deathly quiet. All then languidly find a seat as if the weight of the recollection has bowed them. Nestor places his hand*

	on the gun at his waist. A light offstage drumming begins.)
ADAM	Oh man. Why does it have to be so hard to distinguish between a sound increasing in volume but maintaining its distance and a sound becoming more audible because it draws closer?
CLARISSA	Ask me, they're getting closer.
	(Adam and Linda hold hands in response.)
NESTOR	Well, when they arrive they'll find a nasty surprise.
ADAM	What they're really going to find, at this rate, is a population divided against itself.
LINDA	He's right.
ADAM	We need to get past the pettiness. What happened to Charles was horrific.
LINDA	Horrible.
CLARISSA	Horrendous.
NESTOR	Hideous.
ADAM	But nobody here did it to him. In fact, as I recall, and I recognize it was millennia ago ...
CLARISSA	It just happened.
ADAM	... we all tried to stop him.
CLARISSA	Not all.
NESTOR	I feel, Clarissa, you're somehow holding your tongue.
CLARISSA	You've been observing my tongue in between palming your gun?
NESTOR	More an auditory feeling really.
CLARISSA	You don't say.
NESTOR	Actually, it's what *you* don't say that concerns me.
CLARISSA	That's quite a body of concerns. After all, I don't

say a lot of things. For example, I don't say that Charles was our frailest member, the one most open to suggestion. I don't say that...

(*Clarissa stops as the sound of Drums returns, slightly louder than before.*)

ADAM Okay those are definitely closer. And there's a decided war-drum quality to them.

NESTOR I agree.

LINDA You think they're definitely closer?

NESTOR Well, I was referring to their warlike quality, though I suppose that's not much of an insight at this point.

LINDA How so?

NESTOR Well, could any clear-eyed lucid see anything but war as he looks around? We cry at the savagery we see as we enter this world. If we don't, medical personnel panic something's wrong and slap us that we might better understand where we are, its characteristic modes and methods.

There's no need to declare war, we are war.

In the unlikely event peace ever comes we'll declare *that;* because there, at long last, might be something worth expending breath over. Until then, of course assume the drums are war drums, as what else could they be, consonant with all we've seen of humanity? For ours is a history of ever-evolving warfare and this is as it should be.

CLARISSA You're an adolescent.

NESTOR Me?

CLARISSA Who else would adopt such an adolescent

viewpoint? You feel only war in your heart and so project it onto the world at large. You then credit and celebrate only that which you would expect to find in such a world, while the far more prevalent and contradictory sensory input all around you is not allowed to register.

NESTOR   Judge a man, or in this case *Man,* by his initial or primary act. Be sure that man first raised his hand not to draw on a cave or to point out danger to his others. No, he raised it while holding the jawbone of an ass and lowered it violently to smite his fellow man that he might acquire a handful of berries. A handful of berries. Do you doubt that happened?

CLARISSA   No. Nor do I doubt that several of us tried to stop him, that the assailant was ostracized afterwards, and that as the victim lay on the dirt with his mortal wound someone, most likely a woman, dropped down next to him to attend to his injuries.

NESTOR   A lot of good that would do.

CLARISSA   I agree, a lot. For lacking the medical savvy to properly heal the body she instead ministered to his soul.

NESTOR   No such thing.

CLARISSA   A ministry that may have consisted entirely of holding his mangled hand as his brief life slowed to a halt.

NESTOR   You can't be serious. Follow the history of that jawbone as it evolves into a device capable of annihilating an entire city under a fungal cloud. Watch as we enslave each other.

CLARISSA	And others risk their lives to liberate them.
NESTOR	Slaughter each other for patches of dirt.
CLARISSA	Cultivate soil to feed the hungry.
NESTOR	Focus on the woman holding that dead hand if you wish, Clarissa, but that won't change the fact that the dead draw no consolation from such a handholding.
CLARISSA	Untrue, and when Charles went we should have been holding his!
NESTOR	No! The end of an opera is more singing, of a higher intensity. How then should a life end? Its atavistic mayhem can only be properly resolved in the kind of apotheostic violence we witnessed.
	You seek to paint me in bad-guy colors. Why? Because I wanted Charles to retain his considerable dignity? Charles was like a son to me.
ADAM	He was maybe twice your age.
NESTOR	Would you have me watch idly as my son disintegrates before my very eyes?
CLARISSA	Give me the gun then.
LINDA	No, as a neutral party I should have the gun.
ADAM	Neutral?
NESTOR	Party?
CLARISSA	Unless everyone's comfortable with the only gun being in the hands of a self-avowed nihilist.
NESTOR	Did you say realist?
	(*The Drumming resumes slightly louder than before and in response the four again grow silent.*)
ADAM	Hear that? Maybe Clarissa's right. Maybe the drums are harmless and are coming only to keep time to symphonic delights. But right now

	we are far less likely to regret adopting Nestor's view. We need to arm ourselves and expect the worst.
NESTOR	Expecting the worst *is* the armament.
ADAM	I was thinking of more traditional weaponry, but thanks. There are some thick branches nearby that can be shaved into spears. Linda and I will go gather …
LINDA	No.
ADAM	No what?
LINDA	No I'm not going anywhere.
NESTOR	Oh, will you look at this, Clarissa? Looks like you and I aren't the only couple on the rocks.
ADAM	Linda, a good idea transcends any interpersonal difficulties we might be having and I expect you to recognize one when you hear it.
NESTOR	A good idea he says.
CLARISSA	Do we need to remind you what happened the last time somebody left?
ADAM	Doesn't mean it will happen again.
NESTOR	That's true, Clarissa. Besides, suicide is a legitimate option, cowardly, but legitimate nevertheless.
ADAM	Suicide? I'm curious how you think this all-out warfare you counsel is going to occur if we don't leave this room?
NESTOR	Is that your concern? Don't let it be. The anger of epochal conflict is coming to us, right here, whether we'd host it or not. *(Drums sound again, louder.)* See?
ADAM	Let me be frank, Nestor.

NESTOR	No problem Frank.
ADAM	But being that you have our only gun you are in a wholly different position than the rest of us.
NESTOR	I'm upright like the rest of you.
LINDA	And don't think we're unaware of the rule that says that thing has to go off soon either.
NESTOR	Rules, conventions, norms! I feel such great envy right now. I fervently wish I had your collective astigmatism. Could see only the minutiae as the cosmic nears.
LINDA	Please, refract for us that we might clearly see your wisdom.
NESTOR	I fear it is fear itself that approaches and what is presently occurring in this room is remotely causing it to grow more monstrous. Search inside yourselves and ask if you haven't contributed your share.
CLARISSA	I fear then only that I've been a bad citizen of this body politic. For I have not contributed my just share. Because perhaps you'll call it mere semantics, but I give nothing that forms inside me the name Fear.
NESTOR	I didn't intend to insult, only to forewarn and enlighten.
ADAM	Well I feel lighter already, so I'm going to go now and get those spears, the heavier the better that I might acquire some density.
LINDA	It is a dense move.
ADAM	I trust then you're not coming? (*Linda sits, looks down, puts her face in her hands.*)
CLARISSA	No one should go anywhere alone. No one

should be alone, ever really, but especially not now ... here.

ADAM   I won't be alone.

LINDA   I'm not going.

ADAM   I understand.

NESTOR   Meaning that, unless Clarissa is going to deposit her money where her mouth resides, you *will* be alone.

ADAM   She won't, but still I won't be alone.

CLARISSA   If no one goes with you, Adam, you will not only *be* alone you will most likely *die* alone. Understand?

ADAM   I don't expect any of you to understand; well, there was a time I would've expected Linda ... but never mind all that.

NESTOR   Understand *what?*

ADAM   That even when I'm the only person in motion creating footsteps I don't feel alone.

LINDA   Stop Adam.

NESTOR   No, our ears cry out for more! Explain.

ADAM   There's more exists, Nestor, than that which feeds eyes or ears.

NESTOR   Is that so?
              (*looks at others mirthfully*)

ADAM   And it's that presence will protect me as I venture out.

NESTOR   I see. I think that's what Charles thought just before he lost his head.

ADAM   Since the Evil that did that undoubtedly exists there has to be a countervailing Good.

CLARISSA   Adam, don't go out there relying on that.

LINDA	She's right. If you have to go, then go, but not propelled by that belief. That somehow makes it worse.
ADAM	It's that belief that's sustained us since time immemorial.
NESTOR	I see. He's right then. He's not going alone. Superstition's going with him. Of course, superstition's got a perfect record in these matters. In exultant victory we pause to credit her but in abject defeat we either ignore her or wonder how we failed to live up to her unknowable mandates. Either way, those prone to belief never doubt her grace and power. Nice work if you can get it.
ADAM	I'm not relying on superstition.
NESTOR	Oh, I know you don't think you are, I'm just seeking to put a more accurate gloss on things.
CLARISSA	I wonder, Nestor, what we have to do to get you to go?
LINDA	Not *with* Adam but in his stead.
NESTOR	Ladies, please. Such murderous thoughts. (*Drums resume*) Although I suppose they're fitting.
ADAM	Well, this has been great fun but I suspect that whatever's coming will not pause for us to debate. And it won't be spoken to either, words will fall harmlessly aside. Now, the pointed ends of spears? That might be a different matter, so I'm going. And please don't misinterpret. That statement is not intended as a solicitation of company or advice and definitely not of permission. Treat

it for what it is, a mere courtesy borne out of affection, which is itself most likely a product of mere presence.

LINDA I'm coming with you.

ADAM No.

LINDA My place is by your side, alienated affections or not.

ADAM No, I have to do this alone.
(*He nears the exit.*)
I won't say goodbye because I am definitely returning.
Goodbye.
(*He leaves, the three are silent.*)

NESTOR Let the record reflect that he did not go at anything remotely resembling my urging and, if anything, I could be said to have counseled against it.
(*silence*)
Truth is, I didn't think he had it in him, or maybe I thought it was *in* him but never thought it would come out. I didn't think it would come to term and he would give birth to it is what I'm saying. At most I thought a stillborn-type of . . .

LINDA Enough! Please.
(*Nestor takes the hint without offense and terminates the thread. He wanders away and begins a safety inspection, examining his gun and the sandbags until finally resting on what appears to be a telescope of sorts that affords him distant views. Clarissa approaches Linda and places her hand on her shoulder*).

CLARISSA It's not *impossible* he'll return.

LINDA That the best you could muster?

CLARISSA   (*laughs morbidly*)
What do you think'll happen?

LINDA   Don't really care much anymore Clarissa. It's what's already happened haunts me. And the real tragedy is things never unhappen, catch my meaning?

CLARISSA   Think so, yeah.

LINDA   We go through here once if at all and this is what I leave? I thought you could select a moment in time and become a different person from that point forward. I don't know what exactly I thought that would accomplish, but it seemed it might somehow render what happened before that moment prefatory in a way and therefore less relevant.

     What I found, of course, is that the person attempting to create that demarcation is the same person from the preface. If it weren't, there'd be none of the hurt, and no reason for the attempt in the first place. Link yourself to someone all you want. Yes, it will of necessity make you more selfless, but it will not change who you are, and even if it did it will not change what you've done. If what I've done will always remain, if I can't undo what I've done, then I don't want to *do* anymore.

CLARISSA   It only remains because you breathe life into it now with your thoughts. Every time you animate it in that manner it grows stronger. Be grateful for this matter of the highest urgency that now confronts us. Revel in the intensity of a moment like this. Not because intensity is salutary in and of itself but for the way it forecloses the kind of idle rumination regret thrives on.

LINDA   I can't.

CLARISSA You must. You have a potential other lifetime or two to live. Forfeit that potentiality and the one you've lived hardens into stone.

LINDA   Who's forfeiting?

CLARISSA Inaction here is a forfeiture! Right now we need to forge steel out of our wills. You say the cruelty that approaches is great? Then I say only greatness can oppose it.

LINDA   Opposition on behalf of whom? If you say my own, I'll respond that I choose to enter only a vocal demurrer. That a lifetime of opposing has worn me down to the nub and left me incapable of more. I'd further respond that acting as the sole stakeholder in the matter I'd be acting in a manner that's unassailably proper.

CLARISSA No, I assail it! I startle at your attempt to confine the matter to your likes and wishes. Can you similarly choose not to pedal on a two-person bike, or fail to dip your oars as the clock ticks on you and your crewmates?

Do you deny we're bound together, if only by the fact we've breathed this same air lo these many years? We are one now, even Nestor, and I can no more watch you concede than I can dispassionately watch my arm wither and die with confidence that it will not affect the rest of my body. I command you then, as I would that arm, to clench your hand into a fist that we might better fulfill the obligation of every living thing

that draws breath and *fight*.
(*silence*)

LINDA   Okay.

CLARISSA Nestor? What do you see?

NESTOR   I see him, he's doing fine.

LINDA   You see him?

NESTOR   I see him. Well, I see the image that's caused on my retinas when the relevant light encounters his body's mass, if you want to call that *him*.

LINDA   Yeah, I'm going to go ahead and do that.

NESTOR   Then that's him all right, come see.

LINDA   No, but he's safe?

NESTOR   So far.

CLARISSA And you're sure it's him?

NESTOR   Yup, that's good old Adam. (*pauses*) The man who created and operates this room.

LINDA   I'm sorry, the what?

NESTOR   No, actually *I'm* sorry. I shouldn't have spoken with such certitude. I forget sometimes to account for the uncommon way my mind works, and I realize to you two it will seem like a theory only.

LINDA   Let's hear it.

CLARISSA Let's not.

NESTOR   Which then?

LINDA   I insist.

NESTOR   In that case, Clarissa, I apologize in advance for any incidental overhearing. Addressing myself only to you Linda, I had my suspicions from the outset. I fault myself, however, because it appears I let my affections for the man dull my sensitivities to his wanton machinations.

CLARISSA   What in hell are you talking about?

NESTOR   *In hell,* I'm talking about many things that, standing alone, would fail to budge an eyebrow but that, taken together, form an ironclad indictment.

LINDA   Enough preamble then. Let's, pray tell, hear the charges as you see them. The bill of particulars please.

NESTOR   Fair enough. Who among us was the last to arrive? And at a time when what seemed to be the ceaseless agony of this place had actually subsided and our surroundings were threatening to become habitable.

LINDA   So what?

NESTOR   So what did he do on arrival but start posing all sorts of unanswerable questions, the indulging of which has led us to this woeful place?

CLARISSA   No, questioning is good.

NESTOR   Really? Is violence good too? Because, I ask, who's the only person here to have demonstrated any violence toward another?
(*Linda and Clarissa look at each other.*)

CLARISSA   We were all freaked out, Ludwig was suddenly Linda.

NESTOR   Where did the sword come from then?

LINDA   That *was* strange.

CLARISSA   So what it was strange? That was a long time ago and I'd say you two more than made up.

NESTOR   That's for sure, he certainly threw everything he had into mending that fence. That is, until it no longer suited him.

LINDA   Wrong, I broke it off.

NESTOR	I'm sure it seemed that way to you, and I won't pretend to be privy to everything that transpired between you two, but I *was* here when you offered to go with him and he declined.
LINDA	And?
NESTOR	And have you looked in a mirror lately? What uncalculating male would decline your company? Yet rarely have I seen quicker cooling of an ardor.
CLARISSA	Except your hasty indictment leaves out all kinds of exculpatory material.
NESTOR	Like?
CLARISSA	Like, fine, he was last, but since then he's been with us every step of the way, experiencing everything we've experienced, subject to the same privations and penalties.
NESTOR	Has he? Because when Charles showed true courage and ventured out for our benefit he was partially returned within seconds. Adam, on the other hand, showed the lack of concern of a puppeteer and everything I see from that lens shows he was justified and knew it.
LINDA	So you're saying he's not coming back?
NESTOR	I wish. The king always returns, ask any pawn. The three of us will move our square at a time but understand that we are here primarily for sacrificing, like Charles, when the king deems it appropriate.
CLARISSA	For what reason though?
NESTOR	Because the last shall be first and the time fast approaches when the *last* to arrive will be the *first* to move everything forward, Adam indeed.

LINDA	What?
NESTOR	We're being cleared like thistle and brush that a new form of vegetation may flourish. I suppose we can take some solace in the fact that we nurtured this being, albeit unwittingly, from unable-to-walk cripple to lordly first progenitor.
	(*The Drums return, loudest they've ever been.*)
CLARISSA	Are you done?
NESTOR	Yes.
CLARISSA	Then I don't buy it.
NESTOR	That's okay, I'm very comfortable in the company of none. Or is it one?
	(*They look at Linda.*)
LINDA	I don't know, Clarissa. If Nestor's right we're going to be like a still life of sitting ducks when Adam returns.
CLARISSA	Listen, excuse my bluntness, because I esteemed Adam greatly, but he's not coming back, and on some level we all know that.
LINDA	If that's true, then the decision evaporates. Question is what if he does return? Because if that happens, I must say that everything Nestor just said is going to be at least in the back of my mind, if not the front. At that point we could be like sheep welcoming back the wolf.
NESTOR	Even though the shepherd warned you.
CLARISSA	No excessive disrespect intended here, Nestor, but you've got a long way to go to establish yourself as some kind of shepherd.
	(*more Drums*)
LINDA	Let's just be wary, is what I'm saying.

NESTOR   That's all I'm saying.

CLARISSA   Believe you've said quite a bit more than that but, okay, I'll be weary.

LINDA   No *wary*.

CLARISSA   That too.
                (*The power goes out plunging our three into grievous black. A few seconds later it returns.*)

LINDA   That was fun. Does anybody else almost *enjoy* electrifying terror?

NESTOR   You're only enjoying it after the fact.

CLARISSA   Is it me or has this room gotten smaller?
                (*it has*)

LINDA   What's going on out there?
                (*Nestor goes to the telescope, the Drums kick up again but with a slightly different, more urgent pattern*).

NESTOR   He's coming back, something's in his hand. I think it's a scepter.

CLARISSA   (*derisively*) A scepter? Obviously it's a spear.

NESTOR   Spear? Where'd you get that?

CLARISSA   I got that from his statement that he was going to get a spear, a spear to protect us with. In other words, he was telling the truth.

LINDA   Exactly.

NESTOR   I don't like it. I don't like the look in his eye, I don't like this new drum pattern, I don't like any of it.

LINDA   Will you stop? Your paranoia is really wearing.

NESTOR   I'm only wearing paranoia if I'm wrong, (*he takes hold of the gun and cocks it*) and I'm not going to wait to find out.

CLARISSA   What do you mean?

NESTOR	I mean that he walks in here with a scepter or a spear, basically anything other than a giant salami, and I'm going to put one between his eyes and we can sort it all out later.
CLARISSA	Absolutely not! Have you lost control of your faculties?
NESTOR	What? I should wait until he impales one of you to be absolutely sure?
LINDA	You need more … more evidence.
NESTOR	Could it be more evident?
CLARISSA	He said he was going to get a spear and that he would return. If he returns and is carrying a spear, where's the inconsistency? Where's the justification for shooting him?
NESTOR	How do you justify speaking of justification in a place like this?
CLARISSA	This place is what we've made it, only that, and the just don't frivolously conform to location.
LINDA	And if you think this place is bad now, realize that if you capriciously spill blood onto it then this becomes a bloody place. One that won't stop crying out for more of what it's tasted until it becomes an unquenchable want.
NESTOR	The memories on you two, remarkable. (*He goes to the telescope.*) He's almost here, still can't tell between scepter or spear. You two can continue to rely on theoretical debate and its retorts, I'm going to keep my faith in gunpowdered lead and its reports.
CLARISSA	That's just it, it's not theoretical. We're telling you that we're not going to allow you to kill

	one of our friends as he's in the process of trying to rescue us. How much blunter can we be?
NESTOR	Don't make this a *we* problem Clarissa, (*raising the gun slightly*) this thing's for between Adam's eyes only, but I will torch this entire place before naively receiving even a minor burn from him.
CLARISSA	Any bullet seeking him will of necessity have to travel through me. (*She stands between Nestor and the area Adam exited from. Nestor lowers the gun to his side. The Drums resume, they are close. Nestor raises the gun again.*)
NESTOR	If that's the only course it can travel so be it.
LINDA	Stop! Wait, will you? (*she moves between them*) I'm going to go out and meet him.
NESTOR	Don't do that.
LINDA	I know him best. I'll bring up your concerns, *our concerns,* feel him out. If everything's fine we'll come back together; if not, we'll know that as well and you'll have the satisfaction of having been right to enjoy in your final moments.
NESTOR	I can't allow that.
LINDA	It's almost lovely of you, Nestor, to think you have the power to allow or disallow.
NESTOR	Listen, don't get insulted and storm off or anything, but I see fear when I look at your face.
LINDA	Insulted? By a compliment to my powers of perception?
NESTOR	So don't go then.
LINDA	Can't see how one follows from the other. (*Nestor looks to Clarissa.*)
CLARISSA	He's actually right in the sense that it's a need-

less risk. Anything we need to discover of his intentions we can ascertain here, together and armed.

LINDA I don't trust him.

(gestures at Nestor)

NESTOR Stay and I won't harm him, I promise, until we're sure.

LINDA Not surety enough I'm afraid.

CLARISSA You just admitted to fear.

LINDA But also to not understanding any link between that and a consequent inaction.

(Nestor somewhat raises the gun at Linda.)

NESTOR Well, there's no time to explain but you're staying.

LINDA If I'm right, you can explain it to me later and if I leave in error you'll need to conserve as much breath as possible. Either way, put that thing down as I'm not sure all our troubles aren't directly traceable to it.

(She leaves. Nestor drops to a sitting position on the floor. He looks at his hands, one of which continues to hold the gun.)

NESTOR Think I see her blood on them already, see it?

(He shows Clarissa his palms.)

Why bother to plan with Chaos as partner? See the blood?

(Shows her his palms again then places the nose of the gun under his chin as his hand trembles.)

CLARISSA Don't.

NESTOR Do you find the question difficult? Just look at my hands and tell me if they're awash with Linda's blood!

CLARISSA	I'm not sure, only you can tell for sure.
NESTOR	I know why you can't tell.
	(*He removes the gun from his chin and points it at Clarissa.*)
	I see now that you wanted her to go.
	(*A mournful sigh, barely audible, is heard from outside.*)
CLARISSA	What was that?
	(*She runs over to the telescope and looks through it while Nestor remains seated but follows her with the gun.*)
	I see nothing!
NESTOR	What does Nothing look like? Is it as terrible as it sounds?
CLARISSA	There's nothing there, complete blackness.
	(*She begins to walk toward Nestor.*)
	Were I you I'd start thinking of a really compelling explanation, because I am all but out of patience.
NESTOR	Don't crowd me Clarissa.
	(*He raises the gun at her.*)
CLARISSA	I'm sorry, am I making you uncomfortable?
	(*She quickly grabs his wrist, swings to his side like a matador, bends said wrist into what appears to be an excruciatingly painful position, and removes the gun which she now puts to his head.*)
NESTOR	Take it easy.
CLARISSA	Not in the mood for ease. Explain what I see when I look through that thing!
NESTOR	How can I? Ignorant as I am of what you saw has you so worked up.
CLARISSA	I just told you.

(She pushes him, via the gun, to the telescope.)
But see for yourself and feign surprise if you must.

NESTOR   I don't see blackness.

CLARISSA   What are you talking about?
            (She presses the gun to his temple.)

NESTOR   That's emptiness, not blackness.

CLARISSA   Not so interested in what you'd call it as in how you explain it!

NESTOR   Explain emptiness? How it suffuses everything yet still retains the patina of a long-held secret recently spilled? If I could explain all that, would I really be subjugated at the end of a gun right now?

CLARISSA   You said you saw things, described them in grim detail. You cost us Linda by saying those things! When you wonder shortly at the bullet lodged in your skull you can credit your homicidal artifice.

NESTOR   There was none. I reported what I saw, no different than you just did. I'm no more responsible for the content of those visions than a camera.

CLARISSA   Then where are they?

NESTOR   You attribute all sorts of special knowledge to me as if I weren't just fellow passenger but somehow the driver.

CLARISSA   Good then. Since you're of no use to me except as irritant incapable of being suffered, I'm going to toss you out into that black absence like a human trial balloon and see if I can learn something.

NESTOR   We're all that's left, would you halve the world that you might better know it?

Understand, I don't mean to dissuade. I welcome it now. Squeeze your hand, please.

What would you be robbing me of? Primarily, you would be robbing me of anticipatory dread. Isn't this the prize the dead lord over us? That they no longer wonder where or when or even why?

Please, squeeze.

(*Now it's Clarissa who drops into a sitting position. She tosses the gun a few feet from her and Nestor immediately picks it up. She puts her face in her hands.*)

Clarissa has this room shrunk?

(*it has*)

CLARISSA Maybe we're growing larger.

(*they aren't*)

NESTOR Hear that? (*the Drums have resumed*)

This isn't over, stand so we can at least have the dignity that comes with a defiant end.

(*Clarissa and Nestor stand together as the noise of the Drums achieve crescendo until Adam walks in, blood covering his chest and the point of his spear, and the Drums cease.*)

CLARISSA Holy...

NESTOR Hell.

CLARISSA (*noticing the blood and moving toward Adam*) You're injured!

NESTOR Stop! That's not his blood!

CLARISSA What?

NESTOR Not his blood, yet!

ADAM He's right.

(Nestor raises the gun at Adam.)

CLARISSA   Whose then?

ADAM   Linda, it's Linda's blood.

          (Nestor cocks the gun.)

NESTOR   Now let's see what a mixture of yours and hers looks like.

ADAM   Wait, because it was you two who unfeelingly sent her out there to her death. You think I wanted this?

NESTOR   Yes.

ADAM   It's her blood but I didn't spill it, I almost died trying to protect her.

NESTOR   You look quite lively.

ADAM   I can explain.

NESTOR   Please, explain. But first I'm going to kill you just in case.

CLARISSA Let him explain Nestor, we need to know what happened!

NESTOR   Fine, he puts down the spear and we can discuss it.

ADAM   When I put down this spear it's going to be into your heaving chest for what you did to Linda.

NESTOR   Or we can, *(he shoots Adam in the chest)* proceed differently.

CLARISSA What did you do? What if he was telling the truth?

NESTOR   He wasn't, don't go near him.

          (Clarissa runs over to Adam, drops to her knees, and begins to attend to him.)

CLARISSA He's still alive.

NESTOR   Don't grant him last words.

CLARISSA	Why not? That's his right.
ADAM	(*struggling*) Because he doesn't want me to pronounce what he did.
CLARISSA	Which is what? What did he do?
	(*Adam's fighting but can't form the words. Nestor walks over to them.*)
NESTOR	Stand clear, I need to finish this.
CLARISSA	No chance.
	(*She stands to turn Nestor and his gun away from Adam.*)
	And why this pronounced reluctance to have him speak?
NESTOR	I believe it's pronounced … guhh!
CLARISSA	What?
	(*Nestor turns to reveal that Adam's spear is sticking out of his back. He drops to his knees. He turns and raises his hand to shoot Adam, but when he squeezes his hand he discovers it is empty, as Clarissa has taken the gun from him.*)
NESTOR	You too Clarissa?
CLARISSA	Me too what Nestor? I don't know what to think anymore. What are we up to by now, the old quadruple cross?
	(*Drums*)
NESTOR	What more do you need? He killed Linda.
ADAM	Not true.
CLARISSA	Then who did?
ADAM	He did.
CLARISSA	He was here with me, who literally killed her?
ADAM	You don't understand.
CLARISSA	Make me understand! In the plainest language possible, explain how Linda came to her end

	and why I should disbelieve the mountain of circumstantial evidence against you.
ADAM	It's a long story. In the beginning ...
CLARISSA	No!
NESTOR	See? Only the guilty disseminate. The truth is pithy and direct.

(Linda enters haltingly, covered in blood.)

LINDA	What would you know of truth?

(Drums)

CLARISSA	Linda!
ADAM	No! I watched her die! Address her ghost at your peril.

(Clarissa approaches with cautious awe.)

CLARISSA	But what could be more consoling than a ghost? Proof, as it is, of human transcendence and meaning.
ADAM	Credit not its words though, as death terminates all responsibility to the living and their notion of truth.
LINDA	I know nothing of the dead as you know nothing of that plaything, but if you wish to join them you'll continue disparaging my veracity.
NESTOR	If you still breathe then breathe to us what happened out there.
LINDA	You would have me deliver such a coveted gift without proper recompense?
CLARISSA	Linda, what on earth are you talking about? What happened?

(Linda collapses. Clarissa moves toward her but Linda raises her hand to stop her.)

LINDA	No! Don't deprive me of this. What remaining

strength I have will be used in reaching my beloved.

(*She crawls to the area where Adam and Nestor are lying.*)

And only his ears will hear the solution to this puzzle, that mystery and mystique shall continue to permeate this place, though he will, of course, be free to disclose it freely.

(*She continues crawling to a point between them but is slowing greatly.*)

CLARISSA	You won't make it, let me help you.
	(*Drums*)
LINDA	No … must …
CLARISSA	Tell me then, tell me what to do if left alone!
LINDA	I have no idea, but if a rope comes down …
CLARISSA	What? If a rope comes down what?
ADAM	It's a rescue line, climb up it to safety.
NESTOR	No! It's a noose, don't touch it!
CLARISSA	Which Linda, which is it?
LINDA	Maybe use it to bind me to my love.

(*She appears to reach out to Nestor only to, at the last second, change direction and place her hand on Adam's chest warmly. After resting her hand there a moment, she suddenly presses down harshly on the gunshot wound. Adam exerts a final convulsion and dies.*)

CLARISSA	No!
	(*Feverishly pointing the gun at Linda*)
	Get away from him!
LINDA	Shoot, and quick! If I repent before the shot rings out I may get credit for it. Mitigation that will unleaven my sin when what I want is to

leave at my basest moment. Shoot!

(*Clarissa doesn't, Linda dies.*)

CLARISSA   No!

(*She falls to her knees in grief.*)

Is there no way to stanch this deluge? Is this a breathing organism that sacrifices its component parts the way a boy discards last year's toys? Or is it his reckless overuse that pits us against each other until only vestigial rust remains?

Charles.

Adam.

Linda.

Empty bodies that recriminate against Nature's negligent incompetence like abandoned storefronts.

Come, Nestor, let's bury our dead and remove this blight that there might be the possibility of renewal.

NESTOR   No, the dead will keep, and the kept will keep dying.

Reload your gun instead and come remove this spear so I can re-plant it in whatever has the temerity to walk through that door.

CLARISSA   No, Nestor, the medically proper move is to keep it in. If I pull it out, the wound will gasp to suck death in quicker.

NESTOR   Don't pull it out then. Push it all the way through and out the other end, I want to witness my body expel it anyway.

CLARISSA   Keep it in baby, I'll get help.

NESTOR   We both know there is none, only more strife. I

need a weapon to face it.

CLARISSA   Here then, take the gun. But the spear? You have to stay speared baby, I'm sorry.

NESTOR   Listen, Clarissa.

CLARISSA   Yes?

NESTOR   We had our disagreements.

CLARISSA   Uh-huh?

NESTOR   That's it, just we had our disagreements.
(*they chuckle*)

CLARISSA   Okay.

NESTOR   You're not going to believe this, but it's surprisingly hard to breathe with a spear in your back.
(*Drums*)

CLARISSA   Hang in there son, we still have that machine breathed for Charles.

NESTOR   No.

CLARISSA   It kept Charles alive.

NESTOR   But won't work on Nestor, he won't let it.
(*He gasps.*)

CLARISSA   Lungs won't fill on pride, Nestor, you need air.
(*Drums*)

NESTOR   No, air needs me! I assert that the world needs me, the air breathes me, more than the other way around. Do I have experience of a world without me? Inconceivable, at least by that me. Me without the world? That I conceive of with ease. Yet, you ask me to connect to the finite that *me* might be debased in the process?
(*gasps*)
Will. Not.
(*Drums*)
Let the world rain its ugliest flames on me. The

resulting conflagration will be testament to this unalterable fact:

I breathe through spear, without help, or not at all.

(Nestor puts his head in Clarissa's lap. She puts her hand on it, runs her fingers through his matted hair)

CLARISSA I know baby.

(Nestor dies. The drums stop.)

No.

Oh.

Oh no.

Is there greater gap we feel than between living and dead? Take an orderly century's progression through life, from bulbous infant to vital adult until ravaged ersatz corpse. The subject may marvel at what he sees in the mirror, the family may gather in secret wish for the release that comes with resolution, but when the wholly expected comes it still shocks in its finality doesn't it? That so much can instantly devolve into a nullity.

That gap again. Try bridging it but how? Memory's a poor substitute for presence and though I may chant their names into eternity their eyes won't alight, their lips won't curl.

Then am I damned to be both reflective chanter and sole recipient?

A long, thick rope unfurls from above into the center of the room. Clarissa gently lays what was Nestor's head on the floor and walks over to the rope. She strokes it with her hand and looks up at the invisible source. She raises the end of the rope to eye level and forms a circle out of it. She looks up again and tugs on the rope. Now she takes hold of the rope at its highest point possible and pulls herself up. Her bare feet lift off the ground until she drops herself back down. She walks away from the rope running her fingers through her hair. After some delibera-tion, she returns to the rope with purpose. She takes it and pulls on it gently. The rope comes loose and its entire length comes down around her. She absentmindedly wraps herself in rope until it looks as if a giant serpent had come up out of the ground to coil itself around our Clarissa.

Clarissa sits down. The Drums resume; the pattern, if there even be one, difficult to divine.

CURTAIN

VII

Another Enquiry Concerning
Human Understanding

Do I need, at this late a stage, to even cursorily paint a word picture that seeks to implant in you the sight of a New York City police precinct with phones ringing and mostly weary people shuffling in response? If I don't and you've never actually been in one ask yourself why I don't and whether this is really a legitimate process. Regardless, in such a place Detective Helen Tame walked through a louder than usual gathering that immediately became quieter than usual to enter a room that looked almost nothing like the representations just referenced to speak with Captain Frank Furillo, but not that one.

"Whatever it is you wish to see me about," she said. "You're wrong, wrong to my right."

"I wonder if this Officer Avery might not qualify as Grade A numbskull, calling you on that DOA."

"Maybe worry about your own classification, he done good. Most suggestive call I've gotten in years." Then she said *interesting* but with minimal breath.

"Interesting? I'm sorry but the fancy letters you passed on the way in still spell homicide. An ancient man lying on his kitchen floor having travelled the full course of all flesh? Think I'll go ahead and suspect fair play."

"Fairly foul and causes unnatural."

"Helen no, don't do this."

"I'll not *do* anything, other than inform you of reality. I don't shape, however, to shape reality you need a Callahan or a Diggens."

"They're good detectives first of all, and I'm not asking you to shape anything. I am asking you to be at least slightly conventional for once."

"Asked and answered."

"I'm serious, all that red on the board out there and you want to paint it with more?"

"Your belatedness is showing, it's up there."

"You put a ninety something—

"Hundred-eleven."

—year-old John Doe on my board? Who gave you access to the red marker anyway?"

"It's a red marker Franklin, if you crave exclusivity might want to rethink the procedure."

Furillo's life, and this is not even a criticism, was readily reducible to an almost epochal conflict between two deceptively simple colors: anxious, hateful Red and accomplished, finality-infused Black. Red—didn't escape him the color of blood—spread on that board like a spill. Every red addition meant human tears. He knew this, but sometimes failed to make relevant others understand it. He had twenty of these others and they needed to understand that every red name once denoted an actual human being. A human being that cried when it first saw light, cried that it couldn't return, when its desires weren't met, then later at the realization that it was all nothing but unmet desire, at physical decay and mental torment, day after relentless day; and when it stopped crying, because it had stopped only everything, passed those tears on like a baton to those left behind.

And whenever someone he needed to understand this—that the responsibility was not to the dead but to the living—would object something like the red name had it coming or there was no one left behind who cared about the red name, Furillo would employ various stratagems he had honed over a quarter century with the inevitable result that the speaker would soon not be one of his twenty, so that just then he was eighteen out of twenty and hard at work on reaching a hundred percent.

Helen Tame was not one of his twenty. So sui generis the phrase seemed almost criminally inadequate, Tame was *of* no one and belonged to no group. And that final case she had been threatening him with, he now realized was written in red on the board.

"But where it'll remain red the briefest of whiles," she said. "Enough of this night's black will bleed onto the board to conclusively resolve the matter."

"But why? Why do we even temporarily need a centenarian John Doe?"

"Do you even listen to yourself when you speak? A man lives more than a century, is discovered dead in what is clearly his home, said home is located in twenty-first century America, yet we're unable to name him? So, yes, in large part *because* he's a centenarian John Doe is why."

"Why he interests you, fine, but does that warrant such indiscriminate use of the red marker?"

"Bottom line is not natural, his end lacks nature, so it reds on the board. Possible suicides go up red as well you know."

"How's it not natural? You spoke to the medical examiner?"

"Did I speak to an M.E. before deciding unnatural? Do you consult your cat before deciding whether to refinance your mortgage? Helen Tame, nice to meet you."

"Fine, not natural, but what are you saying? Homicide? A

hundred-year-old suicide? Be real."

"Reality? For real?"

"I'm being serious, tell me where you are with this."

"No. Far as suicide, there's a missing pet cat, as in given away just before death. But what I really want to do is, at the end, kind of gather every possible suspect then dramatically declare the killer's identity followed by a painstaking rendition of how I came to that conclusion."

"So you *are* leaning homicide."

"You're off tomorrow, when you get back it'll be black."

This thing where Detective Helen Tame casually said something like *you're off tomorrow* even though Furillo had only an hour before even formed the intent to take the next day off, and where he was certain he had not yet conveyed that information to another living being, that thing, Furillo had learned to ignore. When he didn't, before he learned, it always ended with him feeling less than human, even though Helen argued that one was never more fully human than when conforming perfectly with the highly predictable actions of humanity. Still, the first few times someone looks at the position of your shoulders or the contents of your desk and extrapolatorily tells you some seemingly wildly unrelated truth it's at least highly disconcerting.

"Well then," he said. "It doesn't seem right to end on such an easy case, maybe you should reconsider."

"No, it feels conclusory, and far from easy. But I will stay here until it's black and when you return the report will be on this desk explaining how it darkened, and although it will be fairly voluminous it will be *true,* understand?"

"Not doubting you, but how can you be so sure?"

"Because I already have everything I need, save for time to sit in the dark and stew on it."

"Look, if this really is your last case, then I have no doubt I'll never see you again."

"True."

"So I have to know what you mean when you say something like that, how you can claim to have no doubt about something's truth when it results from only thought or deduction or what you call artistic leaps. Because the truth I value comes from reports, scientific analyses, confessions, get it?"

"I didn't hear you complaining about my artistic method on all those television programs with the fancy re-enactments."

"I begged you to let me mention your name and credit you!"

"Please, this is our last interaction, don't insult me during it."

"Fine, keep your methods to yourself, I doubt I could understand anyway, but keep employing them whatever you do. If you need more concessions we'll work with you, whatever you need."

"No."

"No? Just no?" He hoped the desperation he was feeling, a desperation that stemmed from more than just the immeasurable loss to a unit whose function it was to identify and seize those who'd killed their fellow man or woman, wasn't showing, but how could it not? For example, one time it had seemed to be only the men of the unit in the break room which necessitated that the subject of various known women's attractiveness arise, and when it did, somehow, despite everyone's palpable fear of her, Helen Tame came up. That Helen Tame was one of the most beautiful women in the world had long seemed obvious, but that served not in the slightest to reduce the shock of hearing that fact spoken aloud then received with universal assent. It seemed unreal, truly, that this same woman was also undisputedly the highest-level practitioner of their craft, and the oddness of this situation was meager in comparison with the experience of actually knowing and interacting with her. For further example, that very break room discussion culminated in the single strangest sight Furillo had ever seen: Helen Tame standing in that very room, where she'd apparently been all along, making no apparent effort to disguise or conceal herself yet clearly unseen by all; and here was the most unsettling, almost haunting, part—looking so utterly, no, *mythically,* bored that Furillo didn't even feel compelled to apologetically address her or otherwise interrupt the conversation in any way. Just saying that when a person like that tells you you're seeing them for the last time it can give rise to a form of desperation.

But it *was* their last interaction and Furillo's eventual exit meant Tame alone in his office, others milling about but never daring to interrupt her, as she ruminated on what she'd recently learned and the possible ways it could interact with everything everyone had learned to date about everything and everyone.

John Doe was a writer.

A writer is someone who writes, Tame had patiently[fn] explained to Furillo when he objected that no agent, no prizes, no editor, no book deal, meant no writer. Similarly, see if you can follow, an artist creates art.

Of the three works attributable to Doe it was the last of these, ENERGEIAS, that was most susceptible to mystery and because Tame had been deprived of the mysterious for so long she could be said to have fixated on it. Her fixation, really, was on the subject of unfinished work and in particular those abated by death:

No less than *The Aeneid* was an unfinished work, one that Vergil wanted destroyed once he was gone.

---

fn. Being taken here is a narrative liberty. Helen Tame did not do this explaining *patiently*; Helen Tame did nothing patiently because now picture the least patient person you know and realize that Tame would make that person seem saintly were a comparison made.

Raphael, who was born on a Good Friday, incredibly died exactly thirty-seven years later on another Good Friday, necessitating that his student finish *The Transfiguration*.

Mozart's *Requiem* and Mahler's *Tenth Symphony* but more relevant to Doe, Schubert's *Eighth Symphony* and the continuing debate over whether it actually is unfinished.

To set the world aright. The work of Helen Tame would almost certainly remain unfinished.

Helen Tame, at moments like these, did not lead a well-rounded existence. Instead, it could be said she attained a kind of fugue state in which, as a product, something like the life of John Doe, in particular his final moments, was revealed to her in exponentially increasing detail until it was as vivid and true as a G. E. Moorean hand in front of her face. It was a process she could only partially explain but one that had produced only success in its lifetime so she objected strenuously to even attempts at that partial explanation.

Here's the partial explanation: To best arrive at something True one needn't always limit oneself to intervening steps that are unproblematically so; instead, a better process is one wherein probabilities are temporarily given almost as much weight as certainties until their cumulative effect creates a provisional truth that can not only harden into the real thing but also then even retroactively raise the level of what came before.

For example, what a cat will do when it has a mouse.

An observer will see what's come to be called play but if so the cruelest form of it ever devised, during which a small living thing confronted by its much larger natural predator will periodically be allowed to believe that everything will be fine after all, that it will escape the violent end that seemed inevitable and resume its uncomplicated existence, only to suddenly receive a furiously sharp swat that extinguishes all hope and that, in its constant repetition, only prolongs the despair; and if you object with a fact, that the situation involves no actual malice but is instead more like an impassive demonstration of nature, you still have to ask yourself what kind of universe abides this as natural.

Helen Tame asked herself. John Doe had not admitted a visitor of any kind in over six weeks. During that time, he had not left his apartment. His vision, so keen throughout the majority of his life that he'd only recently required even reading glasses, had been reduced to intermittent clarity from within a spreading opacity. He should not have been alone.

Such a person could have determined that an intentional death had many benefits, not the least of which would be the abrupt end of all anticipatory dread. Could have, true, but Tame didn't think so: the state of his belongings, the textual evidence, even the position of the bankrupt.

The issue recurred with a frequency that would've startled the layman. Her first case, in fact, was a straightforwardly obvious suicide that wasn't. She had gone from Police Academy straight to Homicide, which ascension without precedent led to many vitriolic memos and snide less-than-fully-exhaled asides, a situation not helped by her steadfast refusal to classify the fifteen-year-old hanging in his bedroom near a suicide note a self-immolation. Tame spent two uninterrupted days in the boy's room before ultimately declaring the note unpersuasive. Six weeks later and the boy's headmaster, yes that crowd, is now undeniably the true author of the note and Tame is ensuring his head doesn't bang her car, all those cameras watching, and certain people can't believe their good fortune when they connect the compelling dots and also can't fast enough seek to promote her insane backstory to the front but without even minimal cooperation from Helen Tame who, when she is shortly thereafter called into a room with that year's version of Furillo and he says something along the lines of *natural police* with her as referent, shoots a terminal look the speaker's way along with unmistakable verbal invitations that are more like commands to never do that again, that compliment thing, the inescapable conclusion then properly drawn that a new but central tenet had emerged whose force would echo unabated thereafter: you do not condescend to Helen Tame.

So if not suicide what then? Tame reviewed every Manhattan DOA that came through and she couldn't fully shake the notion that Doe was the culmination or worse *continuation* of a pattern, but this was in reality a rare mental misstep threatening to form because what Tame was actually sensing was the sameness all humanity reduced to.

Now, of course, Helen Tame was free to do as she wished. Meaning free to say: *very little mystery attaches to a centenarian's death and this case is not* The *or even* An *exception.* Could even have added: *I am still technically employed by a police department ostensibly to engage in what I chose to make my life's work, namely the investigation and subsequent solution of any ambiguous appearance of manmade Death and any time I devote to the unambiguous and inhuman is of necessity subtracted from that work with a resulting potential increase in the kind of undetected malfeasance that so offends me.* She did not say that.

Because, of course, that same freedom entailed the opposite right. So she was entitled to say: *I want to know Everything before I die. So when coincidence connects me with a question of even the slightest interest that is not readily answerable that, standing alone, is ample justification for an obsessive pursuit of a satisfactory resolution, with the concept satisfactory determined only by me; and also these two matters, the great offense at undetected malfeasance and the know-everything want, are related, in that both stem from a great fear, some would say realization, that we are all there is, which puts us in the position of something like God, which is not some great thing despite how it sounds at first blush because of the obscene demands it places on human justice and knowledge.*

Something like that was really what she said and the reasons for that were manifold. First, far as any concern over an increase in the volume of bloodshed due to Tame's distraction went, the discovery of John Doe dovetailed nicely with a perhaps disheartening discovery that Helen had only recently conceded. And this discovery will likely seem obvious if you forget we are talking about Helen Tame being the discoverer because it amounts to the realization that her work possessed no actual deterrent value. So even though she had raised her art to a height not seen before or since, this raising in fact very rarely prevented anything and the number of lifeless bodies requiring explanatory thought was, it seemed, a feature of the universe that only appeared to vary when looked at from the micro level and the macro truth was an equational constant translatable into prose thusly: people will kill people.

Although there was a more encouraging corollary stating that when the above happened the identity of the person actively contributing to the constant was almost always easily discernible from the identity of the less-willing contributor. So what was overwhelmingly required was very little logical deduction or artistic imaginative leaps. Instead, you simply let it be amorphously known that you wished to know more than registered surprise at how many wanted you to know more, although not usually for attribution, until you knew what needed knowing so picked up the appropriate people then watched them go on the record for their own self-interest until the star of the show inevitably confesses with predictable results. In essence, the badge and the sentencing statutes did the work for you.

A monkey could do it, Helen wishfully thought, and most

of her colleagues were at least slightly above monkey. She was free to leave, in other words. And even though to an objective observer her internal state appeared to be one of extreme emotional distress brought on by performance pressure, in fact, everything being famously relative, Helen did feel something like freedom and moreover understood intuitively that this feeling, decades in waiting, would swell even further once she had solved John Doe.

Truth is, Tame mentally engaged in all the preceding because she was in trouble. If something you *need* is dependent on a process you engage in regularly, almost instinctively, then you might find that this process has suddenly become complicated by hesitation and overthought where reflex once predominated. Of course you wouldn't be able to tell if that's what was then occurring or if in fact this latest was a special problem that was taxing you more not because of attendant circumstances but because of greater inherent difficulty.

And it was that kind of thing she found herself debating internally instead of progressing on the ultimate question. So that it was not enough she was having trouble solving John Doe, she now also had to face the very real possibility that there was no genuine difficulty to the matter only a kind of self-sabotagey reluctance to complete something she'd denoted as conclusory where truth is Helen, almost since birth, had a real problem with endings and their causal anxiety and contributing to that disposition to make the self-sabotage possibility feel very real was the fact that she'd recently caught herself doing just that once or twice.

Trouble was trouble whatever the source and it occurred to Helen that, either way, the breakthrough and subsequent solution were going to come whenever they chose and a form of disinterested expectation was maybe called for. Then she remembered it was precisely that line of thinking she'd committed herself to rejecting whenever it threatened to form and also that the self-realization of one's underlying motives remained the truest, most effective, means of mental progress[fn] so that if in fact she *was* conflicted about solving Doe, then establishing that and becoming unconflicted was the quickest path to the solution; only, that kind of self-realization was a form of work and like all work had to be affirmatively undertaken and struggled with, there being no such thing as the passive reception of quality work product. So Helen ratcheted up the concentration even more, although the only outward proof of that was her eyes closing.

Three hours later Helen Tame rose from where she'd lain and almost mournfully walked out of that office and onto the surreal street. There, as if moving through a painting, she gravitated back to the apartment; only now she thought of it not as the apartment where more than a century of life had culminated in a sightless stare from a kitchen floor, but rather the place where a recovering woman had led her daughter by the hand to make a final delivery.

When she arrived she saw that the splatter of the blood was as she remembered. Everything was as she remembered, but what had then been mysterious now seemed almost mandatory. It is mandatory, for example, that all flesh deteriorate. That all reflexes slow and all breathing grow more laborious. It is mandatory that the deterioration one day cease entirely but not in a rehabilitative way. What about in a palliative way? Doesn't the deterioration constitute such a special kind of hurt that its cessation becomes a positive development? Only if it truly is a de-

---

fn. Helen Tame understood this on an intellectual level as well as something like that could be understood. However, this understanding had never yet resolved itself into an explanation of her uncommon interiority, why she *never* felt stillness.

velopment, and that concept requires persistence through time.

Better yet, what is the relation of an artist to his art and how does that in turn relate to this mandatory deterioration? Is the artist cursed, blessed, blessed to be cursed, or cursed to be blessed? Just plain cursed, Antonio came to believe. How else to characterize an activity that in no apparent way benefited its creator but rather functioned more like a just-shy-of-mortal injury every time it was engaged in? There was simply no way to tell, and yes that included speaking to the actual writer, whether *Energeias* was unfinished or not, and it was that uncertainty that had confounded Helen and initially tainted the rest of her enquiry.

Unlike Schubert with his Eighth, Antonio was under no external pressure to create *Energeias*. If you proceed from the notion that there are no unmotivated highly complex actions, then a suitably complex explanation for its creation was needed; especially since there was a sense, Helen now saw, in which the creation killed the creator and this was so whether it was unfinished or not. Helen understood that the trajectory of life did not point toward greater complexity or obfuscation. It wasn't quite the circle people made it out to be either because the two ends of the line never truly joined. It was instead a jagged parabola culminating in a return to simplicity and directness and a concomitant rejection of ornamentation and pretense. It was in this sense that *Energeias* killed Antonio, since someone liberated from Time would be unable to distinguish between a work being written by imminent death and that same work essentially writing the death.

Still, she needed to identify a non-metaphoric cause of death and do so in a place where the leading cause of death was life. Necessary because, here at least, it was not the case that death was caused by an overabundance of life. This was, as she'd said, *unnatural,* and whether such an end occurred more than a century in or within minutes, Helen Tame found it offensive. Because it was one thing to accept that all life would terminate and terminate in substantially the same way and quite another to accept that this highly predictable process and outcome would nonetheless be susceptible to extreme unpredictability and randomness, so that every participant would be denied even the small comfort of a guaranteed orderly progression to finity. Look at the person across from you or mentally designate the one whose sudden absence you would find most enervating, the one that would hollow you out, and realize that only the most negligible spacetime twitch is required to disappear them. Realize as well that the disappearance would be irrevocable and fixed, and if you find these concepts to be uninterestingly commonplace think for a moment if it really had to be this way and whether you haven't actually uncritically internalized something that in truth evinces highest-level cruelty.

Helen Tame rebelled against this cruelty, sought to stamp it out. But a responsorial growth was all she'd ever detected and now her latest revelatory insight was only confirming the almost cosmic or was it comic injustice of it all. We build on sand when we play at building so have to be prepared to watch it all slide down at displacement of the wrong grain. Knowing the answer, identifying the particular grain, changed nothing, but it did preserve the record in a way that felt important. Her report was done and her report would do that; one last time Red into Black. There were moments when Helen still skeptically wondered at the ease of some of its conclusions, and of course she deeply distrusted ease, but in spite of all that, she somehow knew the document was swollen with truth and that this truth gave it value notwithstanding anything else. She'd often, she saw, been given these direct lines to truth but so often what she'd found had not been encouraging. This case, the last one, had been different. Without being able to pinpoint a precise cause she felt almost ennobled by her work on it. She recognized that, fittingly, no glory would attach to her from the work and that was an enhancement. No need to gather people and identify then take hold of the killer either. The killer was dead too; a victim, you could say, of the very violence he helped engender.

How strange how, if you burrow deep enough, all you seem to find is connective interrelation. Learn a fact today and marvel tomorrow at how ubiquitous it now seems, how crucial to the edifice of human knowledge, and how negligent of you to only then have learned it. Helen Tame knew this all along but only now felt it so entirely, except the sensation was not of discovery or knowledge but rather of something like detached bemusement. It meant you accepted what you needed to because failure to do so changed nothing, except to make you weaker when the only thing the universe understood and honored was strength. Simultaneously and paradoxically, it meant that the timelessness of the connectivity made it so personal mistakes endured like a stain. It meant a lot of other things, but most crucially it just plain *meant*. The rush of a sudden exhilarative flood of meaning was what drew Tame to the activity in the first place, and though she knew she would miss it, she felt that the great flood of the last place was enough to sustain her indefinitely. How alone Antonio had looked on that dirty floor. And solitude may help the work but it may also poison the soul. At least it was not accurate to say that solitude worsened those final moments. No, the final passage can only be got through alone, so at his finality Antonio was at last on equal footing with even the most accompanied human. Then Helen had helped. Taken his inert hand and breathed a final burst of life into him. She could rest.

VIII

Final Excerpt of Dr. Helen Tame's
Introduction to Her Article: *Bach, Gould,*
and Aconspiratorial Silence

A young Glenn Gould sat often at the piano and, most relevant to the following, became fascinated by the long decay of struck notes. The progress of Gould as the piano player he was always expected to be was predictable in its conformative arc until 1955. That year, at age twenty-two, he recorded a performance of the Goldberg Variations that still resounds today. Sitting at the piano, his hands oddly moving at almost eye level, Gould attacked the variations like someone barely in his twenties should. The result was a musical maelstrom that seemed to lay waste to the very concept of *classical* music. I will argue that for our purposes, and in a development that is not unrelated, twenty-six years of silence followed as it relates to the variations.

In 1981 Gould returned to the studio, one enhanced by a quarter-century of human technological development, and again played the variations. This time the result was almost ruminative. What you sense in the difference between the two recordings is the prototypical human slowing; the recognition that there are hidden dimensions in life that must be accounted for, that there's nothing to rush toward, and that maybe it's better to elongate things like the certain wistfulness that emerges from the epiloguey repetition of the aria at the end.

A couple things about these coupled performances.

Know that Gould came to view the recording studio as a kind of musical instrument onto itself. Of course, today, the studio Gould used would be laughed at by the average thirteen-year-old clicking in his parents' basement. But it was the best Gould would ever see as the next year he suffered a stroke a couple days after his fiftieth birthday and died shortly thereafter. He was then buried under the aria, its first few measures deemed lapidary and engraved on his marker.

Also: audible in both performances, despite engineers' best efforts, is the voice of Gould. Somewhere, he acquired a habit that proved lifelong of singing the notes as he played them, the effect a kind of ghostly amen to the musical assertions. Of course the reason Gould hums, the reason the listener hums, is he wants the music to enter his body, his lungs; wants it to be the very air he breathes.

It is air that can be lived off of, these performances. Taken together and, I will argue, in necessary conjunction with ancillary facts of Bach and Gould like the spectral humming, they form one of the monumental works of art of human history. In creating this work, Glenn Gould obliterated the line that seeks to separate interpretive art from its creative superior. Consequently, it can be accurately stated that these two men showed Time for the mockery it is and collaborated artfully despite the impediment of more than three centuries' distance and how many intervening people since? The result is a kind of exhaustion of the piece so that it cannot rightly be played again and someone in search of a similar achievement must of necessity look elsewhere.

Lastly, there's silence that soothes and the kind that antagonizes. Any silence that brings us dishonor cannot be left undisturbed but must instead be loudly filled. The time for awed consumption of work like Glenn Gould's has passed and left us in a quiet room, our mouths dumbly open. The filling of silences is left to those with voices but the determination of who does or does not have a genuine voice is only circularly made by identifying those who have filled the silence. But prior to all that, the person with the voice knows, and that person must at all times emit an agonized Munchian scream. It is the plaintive cry of the damned as they realize they may not win in the little time left, and it may seem shrill at first only recognize it for what it is: beautiful in its defiance, expertly and melodically constructed to exform, its notes compose the siren song that may yet lead us home.

IX

What's Left to Echo

Ed. Note: After much debate and internal hand-wringing we have decided, those of us who didn't resign from unpaid positions in protest, to publish (with one minor emendation) the following. That the death of the described individual is newsworthy is not reasonably disputed. What can be disputed, of course, is the accuracy of the contained account, and consequently our decision to publish it in our Obituaries section and not say the Arts section. Putting aside for the moment the lively debate that's been ignited, with animating concepts like the distinction between New and Old Media and what it all implies for society, we'll simply say for now that we found the following persuasive.

OBITUARIES
Antonio Arce, 111, Man of Letters

Antonio Arce, who endured a lifetime of struggle and bloodshed that encompassed the tumultuous period in Colombian history known as *La Violencia* before ultimately landing in New York City where he created divergently powerful works of fiction, died alone last Tuesday in his Manhattan apartment. He was one hundred and eleven years old.

Antonio Ricardo Arce Ochoa was born on February 29, 1900 in Tocaima Cundinamarca, Colombia, in a house with dirt floors that his father had only recently built. (Early 20th Century, damn *present-day* for that matter, Colombian record-keeping was notoriously iffy. How iffy? Not until March 13, 1934 and Decree No. 540 did Colombia provide for the civil registration of birth, marriage, and death; and even then the provision didn't take effect until 1940. Always in effect there, however, has been the Catholic Church and its baptismal, etc., certificates with their marginal notes. It is mostly that kind of recordkeeping that forms the basis of the specificity you're now enjoying.) Though generally described as a mild-mannered and kind child, there was also ample evidence at an early age of Arce's almost inhuman will. At the age of six he nearly bled to death following a vicious dog attack that he hid from his parents for a week before almost losing his arm.

By age eight Antonio was inseparable from his father, rarely attending school (not compulsory) but instead squeezing onto the back of the homemade saddle on the family horse to take the forty minute ride into *el centro* every morning, where they would sell the metal goods he'd helped his father forge.

It was at that age, on one of those trips to the center, that Arce witnessed the murder of his father. As they walked together, Antonio did not at first make the connection between the loud bang and his father's sudden fall to his side, and this failure persisted even as he frantically tried to squeeze his father's neck to keep in his blood. When it was over, and adults had gathered in increasing numbers, Antonio Arce took advantage of a sudden distraction, got on his horse, and rode home to tell his mother and sister; their screams, it is said, caused a sinkhole in the pueblo with remains still visible to this day.

When, four years later, this sister drowned in a nearby river after becoming fixated on and following a group of grasshoppers out into the current, Arce's mother was said to be a shell; one whose death a few months thereafter was attributed, in the marginal notes of her parish death certificate, to an *alma derrotada* or broken spirit.

Antonio and his sister having been the only two of their mother's five childbirths to survive past six weeks, Arce was alone. The twelve-year-old was expected to walk to a distant aunt in Manizales but instead kept walking until reaching Cali. Cali, a genuine city, was unlike anything Arce had seen to that point. On arrival there he could not read or write, had never really even seen a proper book, but he soon taught himself to do both at an astonishing rate. Discovering that neither activity led directly to food, he ran with loosely organized gangs that operated petty crime operations like street fighting, for which he demonstrated considerable aptitude, often deriving significant income by playing the part of the much younger overmatched opponent before violently and remuneratively revealing the truth.

At seventeen, Arce joined Colombia's military, primarily in the hopes that their uniform might serve as a kind of explanation that would reduce the fear he seemed to inspire in perceptive women. He rose quickly, his unlikely pairing of effortless physical and mental courage and elite intelligence something that others almost gathered to observe. The explanation worked as well, and at age twenty-five Colonel Antonio Arce married Damiana Villabón, who on March 6, 1927 gave birth to their only child, Margarita.

The following year, Arce's dissatisfaction with military service culminated in his refusal to obey multiple orders to shoot during the so-called Banana Massacre, refusals that resulted in his death being ordered and his sudden flight with wife and daughter to Colombia's coastal region and Barranquilla in particular. Not a great deal is known of Arce's ensuing decades in Barranquilla other than the fact that he managed to amass a considerable amount of land and other property under the assumed name of Nio de Santos. Nor is there any continued record, or explanation for the absence, of either Damiana or Margarita from this time forward.

What *is* known is that in 1948, following the assassination of presidential candidate Jorge Eliécer Gaitán, Colombia descended into a kind of savage civil war between its two political parties: the Conservative Party (think military, church, etc.) and the Liberal Party (think social reformists). As the country (especially the rural parts) sank into anarchic chaos, one of the few things both parties could agree on was that they wanted Antonio Arce added to the list of more than 200,000 dead. Arce's ultimate response was the abandonment of everything he'd built with the exception of the twenty-two foot boat he used to sail to Cuba.

In Cuba, Arce rebuilt what he'd lost but stood fast in his refusal to remarry, repeatedly characterizing such a move as a form of weakness. What he built there, aided by the island country's improbably thriving economic environment of the nineteen-fifties, was a low-level media empire that included two radio stations and a newspaper. In 1960, the Cuban State began to help itself to private property including Arce's stations and beloved paper. Though he was tempted to resist (Arce generally viewed Cuba's men of violence as kind of quaintly cute) array enough numbers against any man and he accedes, meaning Arce had again lost everything, including multiple boats he could have used to start anew.

What he did then was build a glorified raft with these crazy twin brothers everybody told him he should distrust and direct

it to Florida, one of the United States of America. The waters between Cuba and Key West equal ninety miles of natural treach-
ery. The unpredictable currents and a nasty storm with absurd
swells made the many sharks therein suddenly and mortally
relevant. The best Arce could manage at that point was to make
the sharks most responsible for the death of the twins pay, like
worker honey bees, the ultimate price for their aggression.

When he arrived on shore, after skillfully evading *rescue,* he
walked in bloodied rags through horrified beachgoers to a re-
mote area where he buried one belonging of each twin under a
makeshift cross then made its sign. Then, after immediately and
unfavorably assessing his surroundings, he continued on to New
York City.

New York City in 1960 but all Arce seemed to see was books.
His lack of English now offended him so he taught himself to
speak, read, and ultimately write it. He did this while working
as a restaurant dishwasher, one who was often kidded about
his advanced age but rarely twice by the same person. Then he
cooked and then he co-owned when the owner got himself into
the kind of trouble with the kind of people that only Arce's bale-
ful intensity could get him out of.

From there, Arce kept adding restaurants including some
of the initial Colombian ones in highly Colombian Jackson
Heights, Queens. He also began to write fiction. He wrote exclusively in English and he did so somewhat obsessively. On his 90th
birthday, however, he destroyed everything he'd written to that
point, saying a man should only write that which he'd be willing
to see engraved on his grave marker. Expecting to not last much
longer, he gave away his considerable possessions and devoted
himself exclusively to writing.

In his last few years, this devotion became almost monastic.
He lived alone save for his cat Achilles. The circle of friends he

played dominos and drank coffee with disappeared one by one and finally, inevitably, even *his* body began to give out. He kept writing best he could, often forgetting to eat or bathe, to the point that the few interested observers wondered if intervention was warranted. It wasn't, and during this time Arce bled to produce *The Ocean, Personae,* and lastly *Energeias: or Why Today the Sun May Not Rise in the East, Set in the West.*

One of his last willful acts involved Achilles. Specifically, he came across the cat as it appeared to be torturing a mouse and prevented him from delivering the final blow. He then gave the cat away to a neighbor saying only "I've lost my stomach for it all." The mouse ultimately perished due to its injuries but not before chewing an exposed line near the stove in Arce's apartment, creating a leak of CO or carbon monoxide that soon turned the cramped space into a kind of gas chamber. So what started as a headache that wouldn't end was joined by nausea, fatigue, hallucinatory visions, and finally an extreme debilitating weakness that caused Antonio Arce to sit then lie on his kitchen floor where he died shortly thereafter. He is survived by no one. His influence, if any, is not yet known.

Helen Tame, Otherworldly and Multivalent Talent, Dies at 40

Helen Tame, who began publishing highly influential scholarly articles at age sixteen and later shocked the music world with inexplicably mature and groundbreakingly virtuosic piano performances beginning at age 20 before voluntarily and suddenly disappearing from that scene entirely, only to then reappear on the public stage years later having reinvented herself as a preternaturally gifted homicide detective often called on to solve some of law enforcement's most longstanding and seemingly impenetrable mysteries, died yesterday at age 40.

Helen Tame was born on October 16, 1970, in Christ the King Hospital in Jersey City, New Jersey to Anthony Tame and the former Laura King. At age five, she is said to have announced to her parents that they could either purchase a legitimate piano or put her up for adoption by a family that already owned one. Once the purchase was made, Tame apparently practiced constantly as a child, although she never performed, adhering to her belief that musical performance by the too young was pointless.

In 1986, Tame, then a Princeton undergraduate, published her universally-acclaimed monograph on the proper use of contrapuntal melody. A series of similarly lauded articles then followed in rapid if ambivalent succession (Tame famously once said that "the only thing worse than writing them is not.").

In the fall of 1990, Dr. Tame (at 19 she had acquired a PhD in both Music and Philosophy) performed an astonishing series of concerts at Carnegie Hall. She quickly became the most sought after pianist in the world. Despite that, her performances in the ensuing years were sporadic and she never permitted any recording of them, nor did she ever take advantage of even one of the many lucrative offers she received to enter a recording studio.

Then, in 1997, she announced that she would never again perform for a concert audience, and for the remaining thirteen years of her life she made no further public statements beyond the occasional publication of another article.

The reclusiveness gave rise to rumors: that she had retired because of impending motherhood, that she had specifically not ruled out recording because she was recording, in her home studio, what would prove to be the seminal performances of the complete Beethoven piano variations, or that a violent interruption had placed her on a surprising trajectory distinct from music.

This last rumor gained credence when, in 2002, the NYPD's police academy received a most unique cadet to be sure. Remarkably, this fact remained largely unnoticed until Detective Helen Tame began solving several high-profile, and in many cases seemingly intractable, homicides.

Nonetheless, her silence, at least for public consumption, persisted through stunning arrest after stunning arrest.

Yesterday, Helen Tame responded to what appeared to be a routine death in a Manhattan apartment. The NYPD has not commented on why Dr. Tame was left alone at the location, but she was found dead on a sofa there late last night. The cause of death is tentatively being listed as carbon monoxide poisoning. Details of any funeral services for Ms. Tame have not been released.

She is survived by no one.

X

How Some Things Can Function as Postscript without Intent

ENERGEIAS: OR WHY TODAY THE SUN MAY NOT RISE IN THE EAST, SET IN THE WEST

W HICH is why someone seeking to encounter fewer people should generally go left in such situations. What this Man truly seeks is harder to define, even for him. He knows only that going right, away from the dropping sun, takes him to the place where the bad people are. No, he knows more too. He knows that the bad people, all of them, are going to regret that what little remains of their lives has intersected with his remainder in this way.

2   A giant boulder rolling down a hill will appear menacing and as if nothing can stop it. But should an equal or greater rock come along then it is axiomatic that only one of them can occupy a given space at a given time.

3   And this is true as well of these people in this place at this time. That they cannot coexist together in harmony but rather one must instead destroy the other.

4   So this Man walks to where they are. He walks barefoot, guided by the sun, his right arm ending in a blade and swinging

like a pendulum. He walks through living then dead vegetation and he knows the destruction he carries there will be terrible and swift.

. . .

I N the time before this he had been one of the first to bring water to his village. Back then *un pueblo* was just another way of saying a collection of people congregated near a river. The necessity of water and mankind's inability to provide it mechanically and widely left vast expanses of Colombian earth free of human activity.

2   The first insight was wells. A process in truth well known to even that collection of people but remember that even the greatest knowledge must defer to spirited action. He took action.

3   He dragged others with him, some coming almost involuntarily, others unable to resist the magnetic pull of his will paired with his frightening physical strength, and in unison they worked. Armed with no machine greater than the human body, they dug. They dug and soil was displaced and water rose in response and when quickly thereafter his dissatisfaction with this new convenience rose they formed irrigatory canals that ultimately gave every home in the village its own private store of the freshest almost to the point of invisibility water the world had seen to that point.

4   And during this time it was true that probably the most complex thought that arose in his mind as he afflicted his body with the harshest possible abuse was that he wanted water so the globe must yield it to him.

. . .

WE'RE going to go ahead and call this the heyday of the New York City coffee shop only without doing anything coarse like resorting to statistics or dates. This was way before the country started scrutinizing its coffee so the default result was an abysmal tan liquid that did honor to no one. His idea was to play up his Colombian heritage (even his wildly-uneducated-in-these-matters clientele understood vaguely what that word meant with respect to coffee) to confer the shine of expertise on his new shop. But this was no mere marketing gambit as he ground the beans himself (unheard of then) and those beans (only dark-roasted to avoid sowing unnecessary confusion) came exclusively from Colombia's Bogota, where the contrast between the warm days and quite cool nights was especially conducive to the creation of astonishing flavor. The result was uncommon artistry, especially in the then-embryonic espresso field.

2 Aside from the coffee the rest of the shop was paradigmatic. Waist-high metal columns rose from the floor near an impermeable countertop to end in fully rotatable and cushioned circles. Translucent plastic top hats covered exorbitant slices of pound cake and giant perilously stacked nuts of dough.

3 Most of all, a place like this tends to collect familiar faces in usual spots. The faces don't start familiar but repetition makes them so. The repetition is due to this: lonely people, even ones who wouldn't self-identify as such, can long to hear other people and interact with them regardless of the level of that interaction.

4 Back then wasn't like now. Television had maybe four genuine channels. You couldn't as skillfully simulate company and Silence, despite its far greater incidence, had a more powerful potential to sting.

5 His coffee shop, with its lack of any repelling pretense

coupled with a genuine palpable warmth, seemed to draw a disproportionately high number of these people. Over time it drew him more and more as well so that he often ignored more pressing matters at one of his other business concerns in favor of a newspaper, his corner booth, and an occasional cursory glance at receipts.

6   And during one of these times he stepped behind the cash register to strike its typewriter-type keys and watched generally then intently as Marybeth entered the shop for the first time, sat on its most isolated stool, and wondered aloud what was supposed to make Colombian coffee so great anyway.

· · ·

THE trail of dead is long but Man must follow it to its bloodiest point. He knows the deranged mind of the rebel and how it explains the ghastly discards he keeps encountering as he tracks them in pursuit.

2   The rebels will take everyone, like they did here, but as they retreat into the jungle like suddenly-lit vermin they will deem some of their civilian captives not worth the effort needed to remain their captors and those bodies will litter the ground like routine road markers.

3   He has violated his own rule and taken a pair of shoes from one of the bodies. They cover his feet and soon become red from his blood but with their protection he now moves twice as fast.

4   That means he comes upon the bodies twice as fast as well and each time his breathing tightens intolerably until he can be sure the body is not a woman or a girl.

5   This is a woman but not his. Her neck vivisected by a wide red smile. *Esta es la diferencia en estos malparidos*, he thinks. The difference is that while it is true he is a man of violent sin, he knows this and it often makes him sad. He doesn't revel in it.

6   The rebels represent a new iteration of human evil. There is nothing to them beyond it. No boundaries either, nothing they respect. On the contrary, they seem to delight in a pointed inversion of a long-established moral taxonomy that protected groups like clergy, women, children. Anything that sought to create order out of entropic chaos was suddenly attractive target.

7   So they could march into a *church* on a Sunday morning, leave substantial dead including many examples of the above, and exit with a kidnapped congregation.

8   He has trouble understanding this.

9   But they will not be getting him in a confused or conflicted state. He is going to give them the only thing they understand, savage destruction, and even alone he is excessively capable. There will be no deliberative caution either. He has yet to see a female rebel so women are safe; otherwise anybody crossing his path is going to be blotted from existence and let God sort them out afterwards. He steps over the latest body and continues.

· · ·

B IRTH is less the opposite of death than it is its cleverest symbol.

2   For the seven months they knew what was coming he wanted nothing more than a daughter. He followed all the wildly unscientific procedures required. At his insistence, they chose only a girl's name. But as the moment actually approached he wanted only that his wife should survive what was imminent, the concept of a child no longer existed.

3   The desire to be responsible for adding to the world only a female made perfect sense to him. Women, all of them, were beautiful. Every woman and all of that woman.

4   He'd often looked at a woman's hands, for example, and

been amazed. The same structure that in him and others exuded such brutality, quickened his blood in excitement when on a woman.

5 Beyond that, the physical, was the capacity of their souls.

6 His woman's screams filled the same house his father had decades earlier built for his birth and all he could think to do in response was heat and bring water. The midwife had helped birth half the village by then and she gave him orders more to keep him busy than out of any genuine need.

7 The moment, when it came, was more terrible than he'd even imagined and the preceding hours had given rise to some truly gruesome imaginings. The very real possibility back then that new life would cause death created an almost visible aura of potential horror. The screams of his woman intensified until they were indistinguishable from those heard on a descent into Hell. Also, the violent emergence of a bloodied human form was not miraculous. For him it had become incidental to the larger insight she brought: our entry, like our death, must be violent to befit a strenuously combated interruption of Nothingness.

· · ·

H E said, "I'd explain it to you but I fear you'd start your own coffee shop and steal my few, if loyal, customers."

"Sorry," she laughed. "Didn't realize, just that, coffee's coffee isn't it?"

"What do you do? I mean when you're not making wholly inaccurate declarations."

"I work at the flower shop across the street," she pointed.

"Why?"

"What do you mean?"

"I mean aren't all flowers pretty much the same?"

"You cannot be serious."

"I can, but I'm not."

"Comparing flowers, in their infinite variety, to coffee?"

"Let's do this then," he started carefully measuring out grounds for an espresso. "Drink this, on the house therefore no risk, then we'll continue our debate." She smiled and it was one of the great ones.

2   He started by ensuring that the particulars of the shot he was about to pull were precisely calibrated to produce the desired effect. There was only one legitimate way, regrettably long forgotten or ignored since: one ounce of water (these are not approximations) through eight grams of single-bean coffee at 200 degrees Fahrenheit and, most importantly, pulled for exactly twenty-two seconds. He put the result in front of her.

"Not a very generous sample is it?"

"That's intentional, neophyte. Drink, slowly."

3   She drank it, slowly, her pinky extending naturally. She looked up, her chin rising only slightly.

"I don't know what to think of that."

"Perfect."

"It's slightly confusing."

4   He smiled and she repaid him with another great one. Then she said:

"Wait. It's great, I love it. Just needed time."

"See?"

"Explain."

"What am I explaining?"

"Why it's so great. Remember, I thought coffee was coffee."

"Right. Well there's two explanations: a highly technical one implicating the precise particulars of Colombian climate, soil, and other factors, and the other just reducing to the fact that life is a lot more tolerable with a craft."

"There you speak truth."

5   She drank the rest and nodded yes.

"Makes you wonder how many other things there are like that, does it not sir?"

"You mean?"

"That are susceptible to great enhancement through human craft but sadly remain unexploited. As for you, I hope your craft's not businessman."

"Really? Because?"

"Because my craft is assembling flowers artfully and I came in here with the intention of spending money on food during my very brief *coffee* break, only now I realize that said break is almost over and our profitless-to-you conversation consumed just about all of it."

"I see. There's more than one form of profit though."

"Can I see what you offer so I can get a leg up on my next visit?"

6   He handed her two clean laminated menus. One dealt exclusively with coffees and all their possible permutations. It was extensive and wordy and took on almost novelistic qualities. The other one looked like this:

LUNCH MENU

Soup	.50
Sandwich	1.00
Meal	2.00
Drink	.25

7   Her response to this menu was to assert that it required more explanation than even the transcendent espresso, to which he replied that his kitchen was not comfortable operating at the whim of any customer who chose to walk through the door. Accordingly, they'd drastically reduced the available options to force their clientele to voice only their most elemental desires which they then met in whatever manner they saw fit.

8   She thought that was insane she said so he requested and received an opportunity to explain further.

9   A restaurant differs in kind from almost any other business. Viewed a certain way the consumption of food was not just necessary to but also *the reason for* our existence. Not surprisingly then, all kinds of psychic implications result from the human-to-human provision of food. This in turn makes certain restaurants something like second homes.

10   Answer this then. Would you go into someone's home and give precise instructions detailing what you wished to eat and drink?

"But don't you have to tell people what they're potentially ordering?"

"If they ask, but frankly it's none of their business."

"And it's the same thing every time?"

"No, it changes daily, I'm not a savage. Well it changes provided the Jankees haven't kept me up too late the night before."

"The what?"

"The New York Yankees, I'm poking fun at an accent I used to have."

"Do you miss it?"

"Sometimes."

"Do you miss the place that caused it?"

"Fewer times."

"I sure miss my accent, Transylvania caused it."

"Thought I was picking up some Transylvanian."

11 They laughed and held a common look a bit longer than usual.

12 Marybeth stood and walked toward the door because the thing she'd said about the coffee break was true and she needed to get back, especially in light of some recent pointed comments.

"Maybe I'll come back tomorrow for lunch and order Sandwich."

"You'd know better than me."

"True, in that case I *will* be back tomorrow for lunch."

"On one condition."

"That?"

"That you leave yourself enough time. Hate to see rushed humanity. Life has sped up too much and it falls on us to slow it down."

"Deal."

13 She turned to leave and, somehow for the first time, he noticed a severe limp, obviously long-term, that made her every step a form of struggle. The door had emitted its usual chime when she opened it and now the dolorous decay of that sound, the sight of her rhythmic exertions, and the shame at what he'd said, all combined to form a low-level desolation.

. . .

HE is nearing the light. What began as almost a rumor of light has grown in intensity as he's drawn near. But this is not a warm, comforting light. This is a harsh airy substance that exposes what until then had only seemed probable.

2 When he gets to the clearing it is the obvious site of an attempted uprising. The bodies are all men, former men. But

not the right kind of men for what they tried. No, these were men who gathered in a church to pray to an all-knowing God and men like that cannot be ready for what descended on them. Even worse, men like that could and obviously did draw the erroneous conclusion that the people holding them had a clear goal in mind, a goal separable from violence that served as motive and lessened their danger. It was the kind of error that ended lives and the kind of error he never seemed to make.

3   As with all the bodies he encounters, he feels first relief then an animalistic welling anger that cries for release. He tamps it down and studies the bodies for information about their cause.

4   They number maybe fifteen and they have guns and knives, but the guns, with the exception of one or two, don't seem so deadly. He doubts anyway that they can operate theirs like he can his.

5   Then he sees something that promises conflict. Underneath one of the few bodies that display any sign of a struggle is a gun. The gun is very telling and will be the reason for the imminent conflict. It is old, previous-century model, and has the look, feel, really all five senses, of having been repeatedly transferred from dead to living through multiple generations. This means it was not left there intentionally and is precisely the kind of thing its owner will be returning for.

6   It will be important for him to remember, when those men return, that they are responsible for the many gruesome deaths of people who were doing nothing more aggressive than sitting in a church.

7   He hears nature being disturbed about fifty meters away and quickly moves to where he can't be seen. He soon draws the conclusion that, incredibly, just one person returns. This is the kind of refuse he is dealing with that will allow one man to move alone in the middle of what they like to claim is a military

operation. He sees then the reason for the overconfidence. The *guerillero* is holding a very significant piece of killing machinery, as capable of making a bullet rapidly follow another as any such machine in the world.

8   He needs to think well now. In his left hand he holds his gun. It is not a good one but he can still shoot a lentil out of a grasshopper's grasp with it. His right hand holds the machete. The *guerillero* looks for his gun among his victims.

9   The time for reflection has passed. Silence is required and the gun cannot provide it. He moves into the proper angle, steps forward with his left foot and, just as the degenerate killer looks up, swings his right hand over the top to throw the machete at an unfathomable speed into and through his neck. A small part of the blade comes out the back of his *guerillero* neck as falls lifeless to the ground, inches away from the gun he returned for.

10   When his surroundings fail to react he walks over to the body. At first he is almost sickened at the sight of what he has done. Then he remembers he has rid the world of a pestilent rat. He pulls out the machete without looking then wipes it on the uniform of the *guerillero*. He tells him «*Nos vemos en el infierno, hijueputa, y te hago lo mismo*» then he takes the automatic, straps it over his shoulder, and walks away.

11   Except he then hears breathing. It is a labored and dwindling breathing and it fills him with no fear just dread.

12   It is inhuman, the breathing. A bush dog lays heaving on the edge of the clearing. Through its fur he sees an open chest, one that inflates and deflates, the interior organism threatening to spill out.

13   Whether caused by human or fellow animal the injury is irreparable and incapable of being overcome no matter the will involved.

14   He is supposed to take his machete, he has done it before,

and end this suffering. This is something that is taken as given.

15   He walks to the dog and places the machete just above the wound. The dog looks at him with just his dim eyes.

16   What's the delay? Push it down.

17   It is a thought that has occurred to him often but he is not yet the type to have ever painstakingly set it down. The thought is more like an intuition that every living thing has a required allotment of suffering that must be met before allowing its release. Why seek to artificially terminate suffering when it's the undoubted way of the world? So the danger here is not that the dog is suffering too much but rather that after a life of relative ease it has not suffered enough. Lowering the blade may upset the natural order in a way that has to be repaid.

18   He pulls the blade away and goes back into the jungle in continued pursuit.

. . .

HER entry may not have felt miraculous but her nearly every moment since had. The world is full of certain people like that and don't let their relative infrequency detract from this fact's significance.

2   For it is simply put a *miracle* of this world that someone like Selena ever enters it. The default expression on her face: smile. The wild tempest of her hair with its roiling black curls. The blushed circle of cheek on each side of the perfect nose.

3   But more on the smile is needed. It was a smile could be placed atop a lighthouse to illume troubled seas. One of those smiles that seems to emanate from the very soul of the person as if an innate palliative substance had excitedly overflowed its excess. A smile, in the final analysis, that seems less a property of the person than that person itself.

4   And if her soul itself were visible you might marvel as

well at its flawless beauty. That such generous and optimistic kindness could emanate so consistently from such an adorably chubby package gave lie to the often popular notion that what prevails in this world is dark despair.

5   Understand also that these are not observations made following detailed analysis of a finished product. Rather, these are truisms about a person that began to manifest themselves within mere minutes of that person's birth.

6   —*Acaba de nacer una sonrisa*—the midwife had said, and it was his audition of the feminine form of smile after the preceding harrowing events that began to cheer him.

7   And the world little appreciates how much the heartening the Man felt then was less a product of palpable events then present than it was a form of intuition. Because that's all intuition is: the temporary release of a person from his restrictive spacetime prison to where he can in some sense experience what *will* be true and how it will make him feel and that amorphous and ineffable insight makes him feel a diluted version of what will later wash over him.

8   Selena often wore miniature versions of what her mother wore. Not in general either, at the same time. The result was as if the same person were being simultaneously viewed from wildly disparate distances.

9   Surround the hardest man in the world with love in this manner and the love is not repelled to die, not when the recipient is eminently aware of his undeserving nature. Instead it burrows in to erode the hard stone from within. And once it comes to the surface and is made tangible in the form of acts in the world, it is then eligible to spread like a contagion.

10   For at the continued sight of his wife and daughter, Man changed his relation to the world. Where before he'd viewed life as a constant succession of contests for limited resources, he

began instead to absorb the truth, that the world is more our product than it is an unfeeling location for displays of enmity.

11   The soil surrounding their home for instance. Before Selena, he viewed it as dirt, something to be brushed away before it could sully the clean. After the change, however, he saw for the first time its life-generating potential. The revelation struck him with the force of lightning and drove him to his hands and knees where, in what looked like supplication, he would diligently remove by hand the ground's many stones, twigs, and anything else inhospitable to lively growth.

12   Once cleared, the earth was ready for seeding and meticulous care was employed in selecting and interring just the right combination of seeds that were then tended to in a painstakingly vigorous manner until the result was a colorful bounty of idyllic fruits and vegetables that nourished him, his family, and because the excess was sold at minimal cost, the loose collection of people that formed their community.

13   Nor was this the entirety of his such activities. For he did not altogether abandon his practice of the metallurgic arts, notwithstanding the decided change in the focus of that practice. So from where blades and instruments of blunt force once emerged, more than one observer noted the sudden predominance of tools for cultivation and cooking.

14   The contagion part of this is the external effect his internal change had on those around him. The helped are more likely to then help, the fed to feed. A spirit of cooperative harmony is not created then used to animate actions; it is actions that create the spirit.

15   Whatever the source, the spirit permeated the area, and one could say it was embodied in the rounded form of Selena, who moved through her world like she owned it, laughing and spreading laughter as if such were mankind's natural state.

16   And because her father once jokingly said it was the only part of his body that didn't permanently hurt, she often gently rested her head on the spot just above his heart.

. . .

THE way at the extremely subatomic level the mere act of observing necessarily and incredibly interacts with the observed, so it is true that a woman of great conventional physical attractiveness often does not get an accurate picture of the world and the human nature that populates it. So she's likely to conclude that men are weirdly solicitous and women mostly mean instead of rightly concluding that *to her* men are weirdly solicitous etcetera.

2   So nothing in her twenty-two years had really prepared Nicole Grunderson for the experience of encountering a man who evinced no reaction whatsoever to her appearance. Not that he absorbed her appearance then chose to ignore it; that he literally appeared to detect no difference between her and any other human.

3   She knew enough to not enlist the help of anyone else at the coffee shop on the question of why their employer had had this unprecedented reaction or nonreaction for three months and counting. She also tried in vain to not be offended, finally settling on a strategy whereby he was, willingly or not, placed in a category of people who simply (now?) lack any interest in that area.

4   This was necessary because of the seemingly endless stream of indignities she had suffered since arriving in New York. That something happens so regularly it achieves cliché makes it no less painful for the person experiencing it. So it was with the pain of having your most salient quality weakened, perhaps irreparably, by a change in location. The sheer teeming multi-

tude of people, a phenomenon that needed to be eyewitnessed to be truly believed. Unless his inattention did not constitute a further indignity because, as appeared to be the case, it was his consistent-without-fail reaction to any such stimuli.

5   All of which made the interaction she'd just witnessed so unsettling. Because wasn't that their boss, an intimidating boulder of a man, gently thawing into liquid from the heat coming off what to her eyes seemed a rather plain-looking woman?

6   The sight was so odd and unexpected that almost as soon as it disappeared, because the plain woman slowly limped away, Nicole began to doubt her reading of it. And because a conclusion that she had misread had significant appeal due to the above, that likely would have been the anticlimactically tepid end of the affair if not for a look Nicole happened to spot as it moved across her boss's face.

7   Because Nicole, who was studied in so few areas, was undeniably expert in at least one: the messy mechanics, ramifications, and symptoms of human, okay male, desire. So her expertise flashed diagnostic recognition at the curious combination of anxiety and excitement that comes from a sudden and strong attraction that, justified or not, goes beyond the merely physical. All from that one look.

8   Still, the look and its accurate interpretation were unlikely to result in any tangible conduct if not for a further development, this one occurring exclusively within Nicole.

9   At sight of the look, Nicole experienced a sensation sufficiently uncommon to her that it startled her into a deeper realm of human understanding. The uncommon sensation was the skipping of a mental step. Until then, her process varied little. When presented with novel data, whatever its form, Nicole processed the information by first straining it through a solipsistic filter. So, for example, someone informing Nicole that they had

been diagnosed with a serious illness might mentally note with distaste how quickly the discussion moved into the question of whether she, *Nicole*, might not have the same illness. Yes, that bad.

10   Thus the immediately preceding ballet, wherein every movement and gesture between a remarkable man she'd known three months and an undeniably intriguing woman initially interested her only insofar as it reflected on her to herself as interpreted by her.

11   The change, as I've said, came after the interaction when she saw the look on his face. It was only then that Nicole began to have the first inklings of an insight central to productive humanity. She looked at his face and saw the soul behind it you could say.

12   She saw a man begin to suspect the emergence of a feeling he clearly did not want. Her imagination even collaborated to form the image of a long-dormant flower tentatively resuming a return to life. More importantly, the analytic vision wasn't about her. It didn't make her attracted to the man or envious of the woman, it didn't implicate her in that way. She felt simultaneously greatly interested in yet still separate and apart from the interaction she'd witnessed. She understood, if only briefly, that the two people involved were as important as any people in the world, including herself, and that fact gave great import to their interplay.

13   That she could, in a sense, share an invisible insight with a man probably three times her age who'd experienced a vastly different form of life felt almost miraculous at the time. It was a freeing insight too. She felt liberated in a way. As if a global surveillance of her had suddenly ceased (more on this later).

14   The novel feeling seemed to imply concomitant action too. She felt able to discern the existence of need and wanted

primarily that it should be filled, not because it was her need but mainly because it wasn't. And while true that nothing remotely resembling this analysis occurred explicitly, it is also true that Nicole Grunderson walked over to where her boss stood and displayed a level of interpersonal skill in no way predictable by her resume to that point.

"Was that a friend of yours?" she said.

"Sure, go ahead. Wait, what?"

"Was she a friend?"

"Who?"

"The lovely woman that just walked out."

"Oh, no, just a customer."

"Just?"

"Why?"

"Because you two had such easy chemistry I thought for sure you were good friends, if not more."

"More? No, listen what am I twice her age? Look, table five wants—"

"I don't know her age, but I know the look on her face."

"No," dismissively.

"Okay," she started to walk away.

"What look?"

15   Taking care to appear as disinterested as possible, Nicole indicated carefully, almost forcefully, that *hypothetically* if there were interest on his part he could be assured of its mutuality, and this was done very well in a manner that preserved plausible deniability should it ever become necessary and this process extended over time but truth is he attended to at most half of it, preoccupied as he was with the thought of what exactly the best sandwich his kitchen had ever produced was.

· · ·

IT is Nature, really, that assaults Man at every opportunity. Reason is it often feels as if portions of Colombia are almost a parody of natural calamity.

2   An incomplete list might start with torrential rains like the one descending on him now. It is precisely the wrong form for the physical world to take and at the worst possible moment.

3   The almost biblical volume of water may be coming from above but it is undeniably diabolic. It makes continued tracking of his prey nearly impossible. It makes him feel that the world extends no further than his outstretched hand with the resultingly inescapable feeling that he is in a coffin.

4   It is rewarding malfeasance, this rain, by washing away evidentiary knowledge and burying epochal sin into secretive inexistence. It was appalling how often this happened too, the physical world conspiring against human peace in a manner suggestive of a sick joke. He understood that rain had to fall but that it had to fall just then, there, and at that level, was not understandable, he thought, without the presence of a malevolent volition. But such was the world.

5   Because what a place this rain fell on too. Already he's moved through jungle leprosy to evade anacondas and scorpions and surely before long he'll have to baptismally immerse himself in piranha-filled rivers. All that and more but he keeps moving.

6   He moves until genuine confusion sets in. The possibility grows that any future step will estrange him further from his destination.

7   He knows he should stop, rest until the rain stops. His body is heavy with the desire to stop moving and finally he lets it come to rest under a natural shelter from the rain.

8   His immobility brings on two sensations. He feels now as if his body were collapsing in on itself, ebbing into finality. His lack of forward movement also creates doubt. For the first time

he practices asserting that he will fail and what that will engender in his soul. The darkness of that spreads in him and he feels it as if it were true and not hypothesis.

9   If he fails it will be a corporal failure, nothing more. He looks himself over so he can more accurately predict whether his body is going to endure what's necessary but this is really a performance without an audience because he knows that no matter what he sees or feels he is not going to allow that collection of flesh on bone to quit.

10   What he sees, everywhere on him, is injury. The one he attends to now was caused by a savage spike embedded into his foot then snapped off before he could remove it, its pointed edge starting to come out the top. Problem is, by walking kilometers on it his percussive steps have sufficiently buried the spike that it cannot be pulled out just manually.

11   He is looking at the blade of the knife and wishing that what follows could somehow be avoided. It cannot.

12   He pushes the point of the blade into the red and black hole in the bottom of his foot. He almost screams but instead grunts through the branch he's placed between his teeth.

13   He tears at the flesh that's seizing the spike until he has almost doubled the opening. Now he reaches in with his left hand and, not bearing to look, begins to pull the spike out; the combination of muscle, bone, and cartilage resisting every millimeter.

14   The sensation is repetitive in its agony. As the spike vacates an area that area wants a return to normalcy so the flesh seeks out component flesh that they may reunite in healing. The sensation then is a form of relief but it is a relief of such confusing severity that it is indistinguishable from agonizing pain quickly running the course of his entire bloodstream.

15   When it is almost entirely out it gets stuck. The spike has frayed open and caught on the ravaged remains of his foot. He

lets go of it and looks up. Would it be so bad really if he just absorbed the spike as a new part of his body? He takes an exaggerated inhale then before he can even begin to doubt pulls it out as if in anger.

16   His scream while clearly not animalistic is also not recognizably human. As if the world itself were being wounded to its core and the merger of its physical pain and the suffering that comes with the realization of mortality could only emerge as cosmic guttural plaint.

17   When the scream and its ghostly echolalia finally die away he stares at the spike in his hand. The flesh it tore asunder falls off, leaving him to hold the lifeless instrument of puncturing devastation and wonder if it hadn't better torn into his heart. He uses it to cut off a section of his shirt which he then ties around his foot so tight he emits another though far lesser scream. Then he puts the shoe back on tight as possible and gets fetal.

18   It is in that position that he sees them for the first time. The telltale color of the berries brings immediately to his mind the sight of listless smiles. He recognizes them as the berries the weak people in his village crave. They crave without end so others go into the jungle he now sits in, risking health and sanity, to retrieve then sell them to the cravers in transactions that bear almost no resemblance to commerce but a more than passing one to planned assaults. They say it's for pain but few are left who even pretend to believe that, and he is on record as having repeatedly said that should he lose an arm and be offered some in response he will use the remaining arm to throw them back.

19   He is not tempted. He knows, intimately, what pain is. It can be borne. It is really the knowledge of pain that causes genuine suffering and it is this knowledge that substances like the berries address, not any physical phenomena or process.

20   But alongside the physical world runs the world of

thought and if you go to it for respite from this place be careful you don't uncover an even deeper level of grim suffering.

21　He thinks of connection and separation, enhancement and loss, and when he's done, hours later, he reaches out to grab a handful of berries then, apologetically, moves them into his mouth.

· · ·

For her, the question of God, along with all resulting and even antecedent questions, really reduced to the question of whether or not you entered a particular structure on Sundays.

2　Her husband had helped build the church then never again entered it and this troubled her deeply.

3　She had a list of matters requiring worry because she was one of those people. Thing about the list was that, perhaps in conformance with the human capacity for anxiety, its enumerations remained constant. So quite often a worry would disappear, Selena would heal for example, seemingly only to make room for the magical appearance of its replacement.

4　One list mainstay was the soul of her husband. He would counter, always, that attendance anywhere was not a matter of the soul. That her own belief system relied on omnipresence, so that he was able to attend to these matters really wherever he found himself. This she found unpersuasive. She was smarter, he knew, than him. Anything he bothered to formulate in this area she could eviscerate almost offhandedly. These logical eviscerations, however, had no effect on his conduct.

5　But more than even faith, she was a woman of hope. No amount of empirical evidence could discourage her into defeated silence. So every Sunday morning, once the remnants of the latest truly remarkable *arepas* had been cleared, she dressed Selena in some of her best, maybe even a subtle dash of makeup, did the same to herself, and renewed her campaign. It went like this. First, she would affect certainty where even minimal success was highly improbable. Something like audibly wondering when he was going to interject some urgency into his preparation as the time for Mass was quickly approaching. When that failed, as it invariably did, she would allow some time to pass then approach again. Expressing concern for his soul she would place her hands on his chest as if she were trying to tactilely caress it.

6   On nothing else would he say no. On this he never actually said no. But Mass would start and it was his absence Selena and her mother would sit next to.

7   The tragedy of all this, of course, is that he would've only had to say yes once, provided it was in response to the last time she ever asked.

. . .

CREATION is often a nebulous process not susceptible to easy categorization at the end of which a prototypical single creator emerges. It is therefore not now being argued that he was the inventor or originator of the Cuban Sandwich. Only that he was one of the first to recognize the brilliance of that item and that he perfected it into its Platonic ideal, thereby achieving perhaps Foremost Popularizer status, at least in the New York area. And the first time he did that was as he waited with increasing nerves for the return of Marybeth.

2   But first, here's the promised more on why Nicole Grunderson's sudden empathic revelation made her feel "[a]s if a global surveillance of her had suddenly ceased." *Id.*

3   Take as example the moments when a loose group of people will coalesce to sing the mind-numbing Happy Birthday song with you as subject and object. Or those initially charged moments when you first hear your voice addressing a group of

people. These are generally unpleasant moments, the extent of the unpleasantness determined by certain personality factors etcetera, but nonetheless universal ones. The discomfort stems from the weight of the eyeballs on you but there's something odd about this fact. If everyone, to themselves, is the center of their universe, then why not thrill at the external world's admittedly brief recognition of that fact? The only conclusion to be logically drawn is that it's no fun being closely observed, that is, actually *being* the universal center. And this assertion seems supported by those (the wildly famous for example) who exist in something like the happy birthday situation an extraordinary amount of their time. Let's say they don't seem so well-adjusted and leave it at that.

4   Back to Nicole. If like her you take no steps to combat this adolescent self-absorption, but instead foster it through your every deed and thought, this belief of yours will psychotically extend until on some deep invisible level you begin to believe that *others* attach a similar level of importance to your every move, in other words that you are being watched like the public speaker, and we've already established how fun that is. So now you're this constantly anxious person infinitely concerned with the impressions you're making, which makes you highly unimpressive and you pick up on that so try harder with predictably bad results and those results only compound all the foregoing in a way that's just the height of unhealthy.

5   Now you see why Nicole's pathetically low-level insight (the world is full of other people and their trajectories are, objectively speaking, at least as important as mine) and, more importantly, her actions in response, served as a freeing agent formed in the realization that all eyes were not on her after all; most people's eyes are on what they need to see that moment. She could relax.

6   Nor is this to say that Nicole changed instantly and dramatically from that moment forward. This is real life, not fiction. Just pointing out that it happened.

7   He looked kind of like a forlorn figure. Standing in expectation, ready to press a specially-crafted sandwich but only if a particular customer would walk in. She wasn't coming and he felt more than foolish standing there mentally retracing his earlier steps in an attempt to determine whether he had betrayed his situation to those around him. As is often the case, it wasn't until he mentally let go of the rope that the door sounded and in walked Marybeth wearing a perfect dress displaying a flower print and comprised of what he could tell, even just visually, was the softest material on earth.

"So sorry," she said. "Trying to get away all day but I work for a colossally mean woman."

"It's okay, I forgot you said you were coming back today."

But because the words you speak can either bridge distance or create it, he quickly added:

"I don't know why I just said that, I've been counting the minutes to this."

"Me too!"

They smiled.

· · ·

Now a dark nullity in somewhat human form moves slowly, it does not walk, towards immobile him. But the great fear he feels as a result does not compel orderly movement. Instead it inspires such a frenetic extremity of such that the only visible result is a kind of catatonia. The Figure at first appears as if drawn out of carbonized smoke, but as it nears the drawing hardens into cognizable human features until what confronts him at last is an over-nine-foot-tall corrosive yet inexplicably attractive being.

He is looking for his gun ... or even the knife ... but can't really move ... and doesn't see either weapon ... anyway he doesn't really think they would help ... and this thought is supported by the dismissive look on the face of the Figure ... who calmly selects a nearby rock and doesn't so much sit on it as descend onto it.

—¿Why do you seek to arm yourself?

He cannot speak.

—¿Do you think if it mattered I would be this still?

He hates this kind of logical interplay. Now he *can* but won't.

—¿Well?

—I'll let you worry about it in your next life as I stand over your empty corpse.

—¿That's you perfectly isn't it? Your way of always assuming oppositional combat. ¿Who says I'm not here to help? And don't say you don't need help.

—I don't need help.

—I asked you not to say that.

Was that anger that flashed as the Figure spoke or just a generalized malice? Even sitting in calm, it is a menacing sight arrayed before him. He notices for the first time that it wears an all-black suit, cut like no garment he's ever before seen. No shirt beneath, only hairless astral-white skin. The facial hair is somehow constantly evolving into varying levels of prominence but always consistent with the straight black rivulets of hair that seem to escape the hat atop its head to cover the face below.

—As things stand now, you are going to fail.

—Swallow your predictions whole before they exit your mouth, they're good for nothing.

—Of course you can afford to talk like that. You can *say* whatever you wish. But soon even this rain will stop and they begin to move again. You are at most only one person. You will then want my help. Only I may not appear, I'm fickle that way.

—If you feel the urge to be helpful, go help them. They, not I, are in need of it. Because you're right that the rain is going to stop, and when it does there is nothing on Heaven or Earth can save them from what they did, can save them from me.

—You say I should go help them then, in the next breath, that nothing on Heaven or Earth can. ¿So where do you think I'm from? ¿Who am I? Do you think.

—I know who you are and you can have at me when I'm done but not an instant before.

—¿At you?

—Yes. I don't fear death, I don't fear you, except insofar as it might prevent me from doing what I have to do.

—Interesting. ¿But of what relevance is that to me?

—¿Who are you? You're not human.

—True.

—Death then as I say, or Satan. ¿Who?

—It's complicated, best way to say it is I differ depending on the observer.

—I don't care. I don't want your help and if you try to hinder me it will be you in need of help.

—¿I think if you think about it a bit you'll see that you've always had my help in this area, no?

These words have their intended effect because he understands immediately what they mean and he does think about it and, although it pains him to admit it, there is some truth there.

The rain won't stop. Will it ever stop? He thinks no. This heaven-sent water will merge with our seas to overrun all the terrestrial and flood us out of being. Already it seems as if everything solid is only temporarily so and will soon return to its natural liquid state. Also, a jungle contains many animals and they are unfeelingly savage but generally hidden from view by the profluence of natural pulchritude that creates the illusion of safety. Now though that's been inverted. Everywhere he looks now he sees only the animalistic savagery. Worse, the nature itself has become animalistic with fur and claws replacing leaves and branches. He closes his eyes in attempted remedy.

When he opens them there still sits the Figure, still immense, still serenely malevolent, still staring at him as if, for the figure, time simply failed to elapse. This discourages him and only with great effort does he manage to speak:

—¿Okay, since you know everything, when is this rain going to stop so I can get back to it?

—¿Back to what?

—You know.

—I want you to say it.

—The ... hunt. ¿When?

—I don't know everything. In fact I don't know anything that isn't instinctively known to everyone, problem is you forget. Think of me like a map, but to the village you grew up in so already know intimately.

—¡The rain!

—I don't know. I can't explain rain any more than you.

—I can explain it. Clouds get too heavy with condensation. I want to know when it will stop.

—Oh I see. I thought you were interested in getting at the true center of things, their central truth, not in shallow schoolboy lessons.

—I'll stay on the surface. Too much to do and, like all men, a limited allotment of time in which to do it.

—Less true than you think, but either way know that until you regain strength and more importantly this rain ceases, there's nothing to be done. ¿Why not use this enforced idleness to engage me in precisely those *why* questions your precious science can't answer?

The severe pain, the horrific ambient sights, the utter hope-lessness of his position; he does just that.

Now, a perfectly accurate transcription of the ensuing conver-sation would show that in the beginning he couched his every submission with a preamble like *my-wife-would-say* (omitted here) but that as the dialogue grew and deepened this affecta-tion disappeared. The reason for this was not only the pursuit of brevity by a man who, after all, was speaking through significant suffering but also a result of that man's special personality. For this man was reactive in nature. If surrounded by great believ-ers, as normally he was, he tended toward doubt. If nihilistic rebellion suffused the air, he found faith. This was not an inten-tional process, just an observation about one of the two minds involved. He closes his eyes and begins:

—¿*Why* it rains? ¿Do I look like a child?

—¿Forget rain, why a physical world at all, and why this one of all things? But that's getting ahead of ourselves. ¿Why do you think the men you pursue were allowed to do what they did?

—¿*Allowed*? What a word to use. ¿Who was there to stop it? ¿A church full of soft people? If I'd been there they'd all be dead.

—Probably.

—Nobody *allowed* anything. They exercised superior strength and the inferior were left to choose between obeisance and ex-tinction. Surely you're familiar with the process by now.

—True, but let's go back further to the creation of this world. ¿Did it have to be one where people can do things like that?

—You say «creation of this world». ¿By who? You must be as-suming some sentient force as Creator, otherwise the question is meaningless. If the world arose, so to speak, out of nothing, then, yes, it had to be this way. ¿What would prevent it? If there's nothing beyond what we see or touch and Man has the ability to walk, hold metal, squeeze a trigger, then this is precisely the world we had to get. Therefore, just as the unbelievers suspect, the fact that we live in precisely such a world strongly suggests the absence we're talking around.

—Only if a markedly different one is viable, but let's put that aside for the moment as I see great pain etched on your face. ¿Does that vision hold great intuitive appeal for you? ¿Everything arising out of nothing, spurred on by something that did the same? ¿Or something, an energy for example, that always existed but is not itself at least an aspect of God? Because whatever you ultimately reduce to can become godlike and is certainly more difficult to argue out of existence than your bearded old man in a robe. I swear you people do my best work for me sometimes. ¿Is that what you think?

—No.

—So that leaves a decision-making entity that we'll call God, though I intend to demonstrate to you how little solace that should create. So I repeat. ¿Why this world?

—¿Which one do you prefer?

—Most would start with one where those men couldn't do that.

—¿Couldn't? ¿Physically? ¿Can they, we, do anything physical? ¿Are there no bodies in this world?

—They couldn't choose to do it although physically capable.

—I'm all for it for them, as long as I can still choose. I'm no one's machine.

—Okay so we need choice but He, I'm going to use imbecilic pronouns in the interests of speed, could interfere when things threaten to get too extreme.

—¡Yes!

—No, understand that He never has and never will.

—¿Never has? That'll be news to many.

—Ah that. Oh it's a silly little book of course, telling us plenty about the time's people and precious little of what hovered above them. ¿Man created in God's image? That's laughable. The creation imagery flows the other way I think. You apes would look at anything even mildly mysterious and cry God. Better yet, all your venality and power-mongering would find its way into your gods or God. Fine, the singular form represented evolutionary progress from what came before, just as the Greek and Roman gods did to a lesser extent, but any concern I may have felt in this area dissipated immediately at first glimpse of the unrepentant jerk you'd chosen to worship. See, even your most pious talk and behavior can't fully mask the fact that it's nakedly selfish aggression above all that you secretly wish to worship.

—That's old news. May as well lampoon human science because it believes the sun orbits the earth. ¿You say Zeus and Yahweh hearten you? Can't say I blame you, but curious that you don't bring up Jesus Christ.

At this mention the immense Figure visibly recoils and for the first time his prey feels these might not be his last moments. Not sure what would be best, he decides to continue:

—Because I don't believe in anything, including him, but I love that son of a bitch almost despite myself.

The Figure rises to move closer and the man feels the futility of all that's come before and, worse, how that realization can hollow a person out. The giant speaks through now-visible teeth:

—That's man for you, impressed by the solution to a problem that didn't need to exist in the first place. ¿Tell me Manuel, do you feel immortal?

—No. But I concede I have trouble effectively conceiving of my death.

—Granted, but I was pointing Time's arrow in the other direction. ¿Do you feel you've always existed, as in even before your birth?

—Of course not.

—Right.—becalmed, it sits back down—. So you may think a man or Man continues to exist after what appears on Earth to be death, but no one thinks either existed *before* birth. Yet when it comes to God everyone rightly believes the same thing: immortality in all directions. Now, talking about Time as it relates to God is always tricky, since God somehow manages to exist outside of Time despite the fact that Time is itself an aspect of God, but that God once existed in the absence of man seems obvious. So man isn't here solely because God created him. He's here because, prior to that, God made a *decision* to create him. Let's examine that decision. Make no mistake but that the desire to create stems from dissatisfaction. That means that God, to whom perfection is often ascribed almost tauto-logically, essentially felt loneliness. ¿Is there any other possible interpretation? Because there's no logical system under which God *needed* man. He just wanted him. So he decided to create him. And he didn't just make that decision in isolation either because here's the critical part: he knew what the results of that decision would be. Soak that in a bit. He knew that a ten-year-old girl would be tortured and killed. ¿Which girl, you say? ¡Only an infinite number! Every gruesome event, every indefensible act, known to him, not as risk but as certainty, yet forward he forged. Think about that. ¿Was it not a bad decision as soon as one girl was so treated, let alone the scores of dead? ¿Are we not talking about the height of selfishness here? I want company and I don't care how much you have to suffer for it. ¿It's the contingency of Life that offends isn't it? ¿You say Life needs to be a certain way, fine, but Life itself didn't *need be* did it? Existence was externally imposed on you. ¿Why? ¿Because God was bored? Man wasn't consulted. ¿Know why? Because in all things it's God's whims, not his will, that controls. You're a toy, a plaything, allowed to perform for his amusement then discarded when tastes change.

—These actions you find so offensive, presumably because of your high moral standing, are acts of Man not God. Existence made them possible, true, but that fact can't be used to poison existence, which in itself is neither good nor bad but rather what we make of it. If cruelty leads to suffering, the solution is to eliminate cruelty not to bemoan the existence that serves as backdrop. If you want to see the swift elimination of cruelty follow me when this rain stops, because I'm going to violently remove from this world some of its most bounteous sources.

—¿At what cost to you?

—Don't care, I'm past redemption. The dangerous man is not the one willing to mete out violence, it's the one willing to absorb untold violence with no regard for his safety. I have no regard left for my soul either if staring at it contemplatively is going to allow that evil to flourish. I'm going to do what needs to be done and when all is past we'll probably meet again. Then be careful I don't try to remove *you* from our world.

—Humanity needs more than you.

—I'm not interested in humanity save for two examples of it, and for the sake of those two I'll unleash Hell itself then let out nary a scream as its flames consume me.

—¿For what? ¿Are you that fond of delay as concerns the in-evitable? As I've tried to show you, their world will remain full of billions, each free to devise their own particular form of may-hem. Beyond that, is the question of the physical world you and they inhabit. You say Man didn't have to be created but once created he had to be free to create that mayhem. ¿That doesn't mean it all had to play out in such a merciless lion's den does it? The reason Yahweh's such a jerk is that Man was struggling to explain some truly horrific physical phenomena, like flooding that left their world looking like all land had capriciously disappeared. Now you have more sophisticated explanations for why events like earthquakes and tsunamis happen but you're still no closer to understanding *why* they happen. ¿These things aren't truly necessary are they? They're critical only insofar as they give us insight into the mind of God, and what a picture! He's fond of painting himself as a father but a father, as you know, protects. ¡And if he somehow fails in protecting, as you did, he remedies! Instead, God watches the lifeless bodies float and the waves of suffering ripple out without end.

—¿What are you saying? ¿A world without water? ¿Do I need to list water's many transcendently beneficial qualities?

—¡No, you need to explain why it's not perfectly buoyant! Why your father places you in such constant peril then refuses to clean up his mess. ¿Because who is of greater use to Selena now? ¿Her earthly father who practically clears a jungle on her behalf or her absentee heavenly one?

—¡Enough of you! The globe is as it is and if you listen closely enough you can hear it laughing at my irrelevance. There's no amount of vocal thought will change what I'm going to do. I know what you're trying.

—¿Namely?

—So if that's enough to stop you, consider yourself stopped. If it isn't and you intend to succeed through force make your move now or leave.

—Manuel—it shook its head. ¿You too? ¿Why is it whenever I'm portrayed it's like I'm trying to ruin something? ¿Is that my reward? I'm just trying to wake people, people whose idiocy offends me regardless of how comfortable they may be in it. It is I who exalts the eternal verities yet my opponents shamelessly argue that an idyll is being perverted. ¡The truth! Truth like, no one ever complained of nonexistence. ¿How is that a perversion of anything?

—¿Why do you care? About your bad name, I'm referring.

—Just bodies, but every good army needs them. Mine swells daily but it only does so because I treat every prospective recruit like a potential four-star general.

—I'm an army of one, leave me alone.

—It's not that kind of process but fine, I will. Surely you won't deny me some parting thoughts however. ¿Why look at yourself and feel repulsed as you so clearly do?

—Not looking at myself, looking at you.

—¿And you don't see where we mirror? Existence is a curse and something that emerges from the accursed cannot be expected to produce anything save for spiteful enmity and opposition.

—Again you confuse the order of things. It only feels like a curse you're opposing because you spend it in spiteful enmity.

—No! That's naïve propaganda. Think of the moaning multitudes who thought that true until they woke from their pleasant dream to find themselves in Hell. Nothing less than your beloved two now move to join the teeming humanity immured in that place.

—No such place. I know because I've been there. You're trying to get me to think like my dimwitted ancestors who openly wondered when the kingdom of God would arrive instead of recognizing it within themselves and exporting it in the form of actions based on Love. If we fail to create it that's on us along with the consequences of that failure but there's no place to get sent. Like you, it doesn't exist.

—Insultingly untrue.

—And as for my two, whoever harms them will think Hell heavenly compared to where I send them.

—The kingdom of God may not be a place in the classic sense

but even I concede that it refers to phenomena, like your Love for example, that undoubtedly exist. Naturally then, Hell must also have its own actually existing referents. These referents share the same ontological grandeur as Love and you can intuit their great power when you experience states like jealousy or wrath.

—No. Those are mere negations, powerful only commensurate with how violative they are of the most powerful force we know. You say we're in a lion's den, I concede that. It's an uninteresting fact about the physical world we live in, it doesn't tell me how to do that living. For that exemplar I don't have far to look. You say you traffic in spiteful opposition? I reject that emptiness. So you are free to continue to do so but understand that I am one of those you oppose. I'm going to stand for what you most despise and your defeat is certain if only because of that fact.

—Defeat? You can't truly believe that. I don't claim to have anything remotely approaching his natural power but I will never submit. If the human history of warfare has taught us anything it's that there are ways around such a disadvantage. It will always be easier to destroy than construct. Think of that church, so painstakingly built only to be razed in minutes. Everything you build Manuel, including a family, is built using grains of sand.

—Then we'll build structures of such wise beauty that even our sudden absence won't slow their radiant glow as it sears into permanence in the mind's eye of all who bear witness.

It lets out a defeated but smiling exhale.

—You're certainly free, that word again, to try. Like my opponent, I don't interfere. But know this about this defeat of mine you foretell. Understand that merely latent power, no matter how great, carries no import. ¡He won't use it, ever! Anything suggesting otherwise is at best human sophistry. You are, all of you, alone. Delivered into evil by a truth unknowable to you yet monstrous in its scope. Beset by a sea of trespasses so searching in vain for a soothing voice in the dark, searching like a suckling infant. ¿And what do you receive in response? Silence. Always that lacerating silence from a nowhere entity that audaciously claims to be everywhere. ¿He can't be coaxed into so much as an encouraging word yet abject servility is going to be his reward? Think of that as you move to your death, because what courses through your veins in those final moments is what controls.

It rises up and it is as if Anger itself stands across from him.

—Unless of course none of that matters because you'll soon be turning back to go home and pray.

Manuel puts his face in his bloody hands, cries for the first time since he was a child. He is experiencing the pain that comes from the recognition of a weakness that can't be overcome. When he lifts his face, he witnesses the final seconds of a transformation. The eventual new form is hard to predict at first as the Figure shrinks onto all fours.

On the ground it looks as if a forgotten species is being turned inside out that it might be thoroughly examined for the edification of future generations. Then he sees it is a dog. Of all the world's dogs it is the dog he left heaving its final breaths. Still mortally injured, still heaving, the beast summons what final strength remains and runs at his neck. Best he can do is raise a palm and that does nothing. The dirty teeth look like thorns growing out of his neck and their jaw is locked deathly tight. He cannot locate the canine's neck to choke its life out and the lack of usable air is putting him in a dreamlike state.

This is how it ends he thinks and a placidity comes over him, a belief (not quite a belief because unlike any sensation he'd ever before experienced) that even though the worst was undoubtedly about to befall him what we call worst is neither bad nor good. Also calm because of exhaustion in the literal sense. He feels then he has nothing more to give, and that seems as good a definition of death as any.

Then he remembers why he sits in the jungle, covered in his own blood, struggling with a hellish hound, and questioning the value of continued humanity. He buries his hand into the dog's gaping wound. Feeling around in the mushy squirm he seizes what has to be a vital organ, it pulsates through his fingers, and pulls as hard as he can. He feels and hears various tensile fibers snap and a sudden fountain of beastly blood leaves his face almost uniformly red. The jaw now releases suddenly and the creature falls to his side into a lifeless heap.

Manuel collapses into unconsciousness.

When he later awakes to the noise of the rain stopping, he almost laughs at the intensity of his now-concluded brain fever. The dog, however, was real and as severe pain cruelly registers on his neck he spits on its limp remains. Then Man stands through agonized spasms of instability. He anchors his legs to the ground, first tentatively then defiantly. His hand grasps his own neck as he breathes in all the air's energy.

Then he accelerates back into the chase, certain now of the proper path.

· · ·

CHOLERA, the doctor said through a shaking head and all who heard the utterance, either then or as it was repeated continually and morbidly, knew from experience precisely what that meant.

2   The sounds of violent human expulsion, the sounds really of life being rejected, grew to a clamor throughout the village.

3   A significant cross needed to be built, she said, then placed above the door to their home. Only God could spare them.

4 He pointed out, he said he had to, that this process she had in mind had a lot in common with superstition and therefore could not be counted as praise for the party being addressed. That this was an Old Testament, therefore unsophisticated and non-Christian, view of God as warrior king full of bloodlust but able to dispense mercy.

5 She said leave the high-level theology to the believers and added that Selena was, in a sense, all they had. That she could bear almost anything, but if Selena were to turn blue and be taken that would convert her life into a minute-by-minute inferno and she would not endure it.

6 So it was fear, not logic or anything else, that ruled her troubled moments then. The fear was so great and occlusive that she felt herself converted into a little girl, and you only reason with a little girl to a point.

7 He built and installed the cross, and whether related or not the sickness passed Selena over and she remained the ruddy optimist her mother could not have lived without.

. . .

CUBAN in reference to the sandwich meant he too was Cuban right? She proposed this inductive assertion in between early bites of what truly was a remarkable sandwich only to receive no reaction from her audience. She snapped her fingers near his face.

"Oh, sorry! Cuban? No, bite your tongue. But I know a good sandwich when I see one. And?"

"Truly remarkable, she remarked truly."

He smiled.

"So where you from then?"

2 He said in detail where he was from and she felt strangely embarrassed when her turn followed and she had to say Wiscon-

sin, which just then sounded kind of cartoonish and made up.

3   This was Monday and every lunch that followed that week meant those two and that counter.

4   Polio was the reason for the limp.

5   She was full of all these theories too, this woman. That the U.S. would never actually land on the moon but the pressure to do so would become so great that the Government, it always felt like a capital G with her, would stage a pretend landing in some movie studio. That damn near every physical malady known to man was curable through the proper application of lemon juice and surely he could appreciate the great incentive the pharmaceutical companies had in keeping this fact from being widely disseminated.

6   He laughed so hard at these and other disclosures that more than once he feared she would think he had crossed over into ridicule, but no danger of that as he was dealing with one of the world's great fun people.

7   About himself he said little, though not from lack of pressing on her part.

8   One of the many things she said was that he was so "cute, and nice, and harmless."

9   He responded that "since what you say makes it true at least to you, I'm hoping it will make it true to me" and he said this because there was much harm he wished he'd never done.

10   He told her he thought orchids like the kind found where he was from were a kind of divine apology for the universe's many harsh elements and she later brought him some, which made him feel more than a little weird.

11   Not possible, she said, based on the visual evidence, that he had put that many years into life. And look at herself which led to a brief detour into the subject of Nicole Grunderson and her like. He said, with a complete absence of flattery intent, that

the difference between a *woman*—one who had lived, suffered, learned, wept, transitorily gained then lost, faced death, bowed from pressure, then been scarred by all that into steel—and a shiny *girl* was one of the great chasms in life and he'd let her deduce which was preferable. Me? Little more than scar tissue.

12 On the Friday, she stayed right through to dinnertime, at which point he declared he couldn't bear even the sight of his own food anymore so they walked the few blocks to a new Italian restaurant receiving mountainous praise though it turned out undeservedly so.

13 Afterwards, she needed to reclaim the many blocks that had accumulated between the disappointing restaurant and her studio apartment not helped by a frigid air that moved in while they ate yet solely through the use of body language and in perfect synchronicity they decided to eschew the many available taxis and walk the space during which walk Marybeth felt completely and utterly protected and she and her protector slowly then quickly drew closer to each other until her really exceptionally lovely hand extended away from her body where he clasped it quickly as if trying to convince himself that his action had been reflexive and not the product of even minimal aforethought then those hands swung rhythmically as if winding the couple to their destination until stopping because they were there where Marybeth wondered aloud if he might not come up and maybe overcome his prejudice against tea but after starting to form assent he suddenly remembered himself and declined in a manner that in no way offended Marybeth who also wasn't the least bit surprised by a demurral that seemed to inappositely build as the week and their intimacy progressed and also there was the matter of her early rise the next morning for that weekend thing they'd discussed so that from within a hug they agreed to resume whatever this was the following Monday.

14   He stood alone on the sidewalk. It was dark as the city was allowed to get. He stared intently at the window. The light came on. She was safe. He left.

· · ·

L ORD grant me the strength to decimate into dust your transgressing sons that such sensational cruelty will echo throughout the ages and discourage future transgressors into obedience.

2   This is the kind of illogic Manuel finds escaping his mouth as he grinds himself up the hill in what feels like at most half a body.

3   This is Skull Hill, so named because of the peculiar rock formation at its summit that creates the not just visual impression that a malevolent giant once died there then all but its skull decomposed into the form of a hill.

4   Thing about the hill is that it's a lot steeper than it looked on approach and he now doubts very much that he will later descend it. Already he has fallen badly twice and each time a dispassionate observer would not have wagered he would rise again as he did.

5   At the top, it is rumored, is a mass grave. Almost certainly not true at the time of the rumors but probably so now.

6   He feels as if there couldn't possibly be any blood left inside him but also the remarkable realization that he never really needed blood to begin with.

7   The disturbance caused by even silent people is unlike any other so he's not even mildly surprised when he looks through some jungle and sees the goal he's suffered for available like ripe fruit fallen from its tree.

8   He cannot see them but they must be there among the group. They are there because he left them alone, and when he's

done what he came to do they will likely be alone again because right now to him his life means not next to nothing, goddamn less than nothing.

9   He will deliver it up sacrificially but they will walk away unharmed to resume their lives, his absence rightly weakening daily.

· · ·

FIRST sign of trouble came from the human wailing, not the sound of gunfire which one grew accustomed to coming from the jungle.

2   The church was close enough that, although too late to prevent anything, Manuel was able to arrive before any diminution in the screams.

3   For the irreligious, understand that there's a moment in the Catholic service in which all present are asked to demonstrate peace towards each other, usually in the form of a handshake although more is permitted within reason. Coincidentally or not, this was the moment they burst in, every opening covered, barking contradictory orders that couldn't possibly be complied with before bullets took apocalyptic flights through the still air, first disproportionately into the celebrant then randomly into the congregation, where Luz smothered Selena in protection, willing that all the world's steel should be embedded in her body rather than reach her daughter's innocence.

4   One could view the quickly dead as the lucky, as dozens of others are forcibly pushed and pulled into the jungle as if tethered to guns still warm from their displays. These are the people whose physical lives have become so suddenly and dramatically constricted that they must retreat into a purely mental existence, and it's a torturous one for the reason that the worst part about a death sentence is the waiting in expectation. Luz and Selena are

in this group and before it even seems possible time-wise this group is in the jungle.

5 When Manuel arrived he understood almost instantaneously what had occurred. He displayed no emotion but did very little breathing as he walked among the bloody dead, touching them only when necessary to see their blank deanimated faces.

6 When the pointless police and some military arrived, he did not look to them for help. Instead, he stood unobtrusively by as witnesses spoke so he could gain the information he needed.

7 Then he went into the jungle to get his wife and daughter back, the only two things of value he'd ever had in this accursed world.

. . .

S MILES come in many different forms so the following Monday when Marybeth entered the coffee shop she did smile when their eyes met but it was the kind you might see at a funeral.

2 The explanation? Cancer she said. Spreading through her sister like … Cancer.

3 And probably the thing her sister was worst at, her whole life, was the selection of men, so that it took only cancerous rumors for her husband to flee their two single-digit children into her care.

4 She would go and do her best, this wasn't really who she was.

5 You'll be who you choose to be, he said, and his mere declaration made it seem probably true to her.

6 She hoped to return soon. He hoped that too. Wisconsin wasn't all that far away and really considered the jewel of these united states if he was curious.

7 He could take her to the airport, but one thing:

"Just promise you'll let her partake of conventional medicine in addition to your lemon treatments."

. . .

I N the beginning was such simplicity. As a child he learned to track human movement through jungle and the movement of so many was particularly simple. They moved, he moved in pursuit, and the distance between them, he knew, closed with each step.

2   Now the steps require deliberation. They are ten. Seven of them have guns. They have other weapons but guns are all he bothers to count.

3   They hold probably twenty. Of those tearful twenty at least his two will soon be free. He is thinking of how.

4   The layout is good. He is on one side of them but can with relative ease move to the opposite side undetected.

5   He creates an intentional disturbance to the side of where he stands and expects two of the ten to respond. He is right. The two have guns but no real chance. Before they can even begin to understand the situation, their necks are open, they lie in pooling blood, and their emptied guns have been left at their side as last earthly reward.

6   He expects one more and he is right again. Before that one can scream his grim discovery, he has joined it.

7   Manuel now moves to the opposite end and waits, won't be long. He senses an electric tension among the seven, dim at first then rising in intensity as they rightly suspect their cohorts won't be returning. The seven are at attention, four of them caressing guns like reunited lovers. They stupidly stare in the direction of the disappeared.

8   Manuel identifies the one with the best gun and the first non-human noise heard in a while is the sound of multiple bul-

lets dismembering this individual before he can even turn and face their source. The other three turn and start firing indiscriminately. Man puts one between the eyes of the most dangerous shooter but before he can move to the next he receives a bullet to his chest with such force that it spins him away from his targets. Another bullet, this one to his leg, drops him to the ground where he crawls to a rock for cover but not before discharging one more fatal shot with his left hand after his automatic fails.

9   This becomes a bit of a standoff. Manuel firing and being fired upon from behind a rock. But when he hears his opponent instruct his others to go kill the hostages, Man rises and walks right to the declarant taking two bullets to deliver the last one needed.

10   The ensuing is even less pretty than what came before, as Manuel follows the three until he can establish conclusively that the hostages are not in immediate danger. Then, receiving only a vicious dagger to his side, he eliminates them with his bare hands.

11   His death is almost certain now, he feels, and there is just one more earthly sight he wishes to see. He is looking through the hostages, now free, and they fear him. He looks directly into the eyes of a familiar girl. Her face functions as a kind of mirror just then and the reflection somehow unsettles him more than what immediately preceded it.

«¿La niña? ¿Mi niña?» He almost describes her smile then remembers they were unlikely to have seen it. «¿Luz y Selena?» They had bonded, of course, and knew each other by name.

12   Luz and Selena were part of a small group, they say, that went ahead to shelter when the storm hit. There is more, but they are hesitant to continue and even if they weren't, they aren't sure of anything.

13   He covers the two kilometers as if he weren't dying. To-

wards the end, he falls terribly. He melts into the ground as if the universe itself were burying him, one less son to worry.

14 But he rises, he always rises this Man. Problem is he rises into an enervating discovery. A windowless structure, its remains. A scorched fallen tree lies across and blocking what was the door.

15 It takes some time to figure it out. He doesn't want to. The smoldering remains of a dozen bodies. The structure reduced to random beams of carbon.

16 Lightning. Lightning struck a tree that then lit up as it fell, blocking the only possible exit from a box containing three sons of diseased whores caging twelve hostages there. All were consumed alive in the resulting conflagration that must have felt as if Hell itself had risen up through the ground to make an end of everything. Impersonal lightning. The highly flammable nature of wood. No human will involved.

17 He surveys the dead, the charred bodies. And this is where it gets odd, because Manuel makes sure to avoid a conclusive identification of any of them. Although, if looking down from above, you would witness a great suffering as he stands in the vicinity of what appears to be the remnants of a woman enveloping a young girl.

18 He must continue the search for Luz and Selena, but first he will demonstrate respect for the dead by burying only the hostages. He has little remaining strength so he buries only this woman and girl, careful not to look at their faces.

19 Luz is like him, made of steel. She will not let harm come to all they have.

20 The woman and girl are together and covered by dirt. Manuel says, in words that enter the air then are diluted by it into silence, never to be heard by fellow human, that he will continue his search. But first he must rest.

21 He lays on the dirt above them, face and bullet-filled chest down. He says he cannot be blamed for his own death. He cannot resist anymore. A lifetime of resistance. Flesh famously devolves but so can a soul. His is mortally wounded.

22 The blood from his chest enters the dirt and converts it into soil. It is what the universe unapologetically demands and he deliriously accedes. That our very essence must merge with the dead. That life must continuously arise in response only to meet a violent terminus. It is a story years in the telling, billions, and it is a story without end.

· · ·

HERE *he says Yes maybe he always says Yes Whatever the case they stand (the three of them) in a melodic church And when the moment comes for exchanging peace Manuel and Luz hug with Selena sandwiched between He feels this hug not only as real as anything he's ever felt but somehow more real Nothing foreign comes through the church door and Mass just ends Back home Man and Luz garden while nearby Selena plays benevolent Queen to a congregation of handcrafted dolls The sun above them warms without scorching and the air smells maybe slightly sweet.*

· · ·

NOTHING romantically cute happened at the airport. He just watched her airplane shrink from a giant winged god into a tiny metal speck the sky suddenly chose to blot out. He decided he should listen to live music that night and he was certainly the oldest person to have made that decision where he found himself. Raised on endless clave patterns, he'd only recently come to appreciate drums and two kinds of guitar, and there was a moment where it seemed this latest iteration of Music might finally fuse Heaven and Earth, but this was a misconception based on the fact that its greatest practitioners appeared near the outset then were never surpassed.

2   Still, this became an incredibly fertile time, so that even a band with the limited appeal of the one then playing would create music that still echoes forcefully today. They wrote mostly dark songs depicting seamy NYC life but one that night was exceptional. Built on verses that functioned more like incantatory refrains and plaintive yet defiant guitar, they sang that every human being, no matter how seemingly inconsequential, should at some point have breath expended on its behalf.

3   He felt a weak joy, not so much at the particulars of the song, great as they were, as at the mere fact it was ever created, if that makes any sense. Near the end, the singer seemed to grow frustrated with the limits of his words and in an expert reversal of Beethoven's Ninth expressed the brotherhood of Man more cogently through an electric guitar's wail that leveled everyone present. The world had shrunk.

4   None of which is to say that when he got home that night he didn't feel the cruel fact that no one needed to be told of his arrival.

. . .

SURPRISE is the sensation he most experiences upon his return to the living. Until he realizes that his life, at least its continued existence, makes perfect sense. Imprisonment is for the guilty, natural release for the innocent or reformed. He suspects he'll live forever.

2   On the away he encounters another soul. Its uniform places it in imminent mortal danger, a truth it seems to intuit on first sight of Manuel, so it states in defense that it is unarmed. Man is thinking lightning may have been at direct fault, but

they were only in its path because of that uniform. He points his blade at the uniform. Then suddenly he flips it in his hand and tosses it handle-first to his opponent as if to say *arm yourself if you know what's good for you because even though I am now unarmed and savagely beaten I remain capable of great wrath*. When his opponent reacts by moving toward the blade, Manuel begins to close the distance between them. But the opponent doesn't pick up the blade. He sees what's coming, turns, and runs away.

    3   Manuel does pick it up. He raises it high over his head. He throws it with all his remaining force, but this time when he does so it is into the ground near his feet. To the extent that kind of act ever made any sense, it makes none in the name of Selena. The blade sticks out upright, like a cross, and he half expects it to cleave the globe in half. Once loosed all the world's core of bilious hateful hurt can escape like a geyser. Color the world black, the only way back to the light. Or can he just absorb it all on behalf of its Lights and Selenas? Have it grind his bones into meal and boil his blood until it consumes all his incarcerative flesh. But the blade just sticks out dumbly. More silence, the currency of the world. The emptying nonentity that feeds no one, sustains nothing. He can pull the bullets out of his body and said body will heal its many tears but that dispiriting general quietude will still prevail. He screams just to pierce it, to assert opposition. He falls to his knees and looks skyward. He did not expect to have to make any more decisions. He looks down then slumps forward into indefinition. At any given moment you are either doing something or you are something's victim. He stands and walks. He must, he decides, continue his search. He knows, maybe, where to begin.

Come down to the River honey.

Its diaphanous water and it's diaphanous water can salve your wounds.

Leave me with nothing, expect nothing in return.

Nothing leaves, no extinction only transformation.

Then will you come to raise the dead?

Because the rain falls on the living and the dead alike and its cyclic fall is neverending.

Come, down to the River.

No valley so deep it can't be filled when, in final aggregate, every mountain plus time equals a molehill.

Do you feel how we're brothers and sisters yet your brother turns away in fear?

How, once impelled, wrath must eat its way out from within to be expelled.

Yet even the loneliest flower is arrayed in hues so beautiful it can out of thorn and thistle the loveliest meadow make.

Come to the River.

The Sun, up and down, up and down, but what if next time it refuse to rise?

The Human Tragicomedy, the spark of life may blaze

sequentially but it can also flicker perilously or suddenly extinguish, leaving only a dark chill.

Stare, at the abyss, at the speck in your brother's eye, at infirmity and loss, until your failure to turn away leave you blind as a pillar and blindness is general.

Immerse yourself, your self, in the River and wade in its water.

Excavate the ruinous to sort the living from the dead then determine if it is life that can be lived on.

I prey that I might be shown the way and it is a grueling, confusing dissent.

To the River and out of harm.

Rage at the infinite and eternal, spirited solace for the sick to bear their burden.

Come to the eternal River, come.

Come children. Where the fish drink and drink to nascent love. Then. Once the water's restored you. Lay back and float. As you lay, Living, the current will raise you. Truth ascends, lies stay stuck on the ground. Stare so intently at the sky, Heaven's gates begin to almost imperceptibly part. Then draw in some air honey. Sweet air. And let the current bear you home.

New York, NY
March 2011